Praise for *Descriptions of Heaven*

"Descriptions of Heaven is an admirable sort of quietly suspenseful literary novel; its prose flows without awkwardness, and heartrending gothic secrets are revealed in due course as the philosophical narrative unfolds."

—Kevin Polman, author of *The Extra Key*

"From the very first pages, I saw the lives of these characters like a shattering mirror. All those details which make everyday life normal will be torn apart in front of the characters, leaving them unable to do anything but wait for that final dreaded moment and afterwards try to move on."

—*eLitere*

"I loved the author's prose and his style in general. Greene makes poetry of his prose and commands the page. For that reason alone, it was a joy to read."

—*The Underground*

"Let yourself get involved, and you may be pulled in by the linguist's efforts to use the tools of his craft—words—as aids in his search for answers to his son's (and his own) questions about why Natalia is dying and where she is going."

—*IndieReader*

"What's surprised me is how such a short book has left lasting thoughts. Greene's use of words has evoked such vivid images and thoughts that I find I'm contemplating life and death myself. An interesting and thought-provoking read."

—*Happymeerkatreviews*

"With so many hauntingly beautiful lines, and characters that I cared about and became attached to, I felt as if I, too, took this journey, and I've been changed along with them. And for me, that's the ultimate gift that a story could give."

—*Unbroken Journal*

Descriptions of Heaven

Randal Eldon Greene

Harvard Square Editions
New York
2016

ISBN 978-1-941861-27-1
Printed in the United States of America

Published in the United States by
Harvard Square Editions
www.harvardsquareeditions.org

To my grandmother, Lydia Saltsgiver
December 23, 1934–January 25, 2014

It is difficult for those whose thoughts are habitually employed about sensible things to conceive of spiritual truths, and the difficulty is increased by the circumstance that the language in which they are expressed was at first materialistic, and is still apt to call up sensible images.

—*Dr. James McCosh*

1

THEY CRASHED THROUGH THE REEDS, and they left deep ruts cut into the soft and mossy earth there on the banks of the New Bedford Lake. Their vans were all white with the names of news stations emblazoned on the sides and mini satellite dishes wired to the roofs. My son eagerly watched the last of the camera crews standing in the wet air that spit cold drops on their reporter. The reporter was a blond man I recognized from the Midway News team, meaning that this would at least be broadcast statewide. He, like all the reporters, wore a raincoat. His was yellow, and his red face beamed as he spoke into the microphone, making large gestures with his other arm toward the water, which, on that day, appeared gray and menacing behind him.

"They're almost done," Jesse said, turning away from the window to look at me.

"Okay," I replied. He wanted me to get on my shoes, my raincoat, and my hat.

I looked at my wife. She sat in a rocking chair, a cup of steaming homemade mocha I had prepared was in her hands. Her gaze turned inward, at her own thoughts. Finally, she saw me looking at her.

"Go." She smiled at me. She knew I did not want to leave her. She moved her hair behind her ear and sipped at her drink. I had not yet gotten used to the dark shade of brown that her hair was then.

When the camera crew left, we went outside. I followed my son, who ran ahead of me. He reached the edge of our yard on the banks of the lake and stood on a rock, and he looked out into the water with the hope of seeing the lake monster. It was caught on camera by a young couple filming in an adjacent lot where only sedge and woodoats grew, and where the news crews kept coming in all that morning. They had filmed it Friday, just the day before, and the video had spread in those few hours across the infoscapes of the Web, for even I had heard in an email about the sighting in the water. My friend asked if it was near me. After watching the video, gone viral on the Net, I replied that, yes, the event played out pretty much in my backyard.

The clip showed an attractive young woman waving at the camera. She had long nails painted apricot color and big white teeth. The camera operator, in a male voice, said, "Hey look," and the camera zoomed in on the water and shook as he ran forward. There were a few blurred seconds of video as the camera refocused. Surfacing from the water were three humps, much like other archetypal footage from years past at other lakes. The video, though, did take a unique turn, one that aroused wonder even in my skeptical joints. The humps seemed to rotate and began to submerge and then, in front of them, something brown and large ascended out of the water, dripping and wet, thin and pear-shaped—really resembling a large fin—then, quickly, it splashed back into the water, sending up waves and droplets and, finally, left a ring rippling in the lake where the creature, or hoax, had been.

I looked back at our house. The picture window reflected the gray haze of the sky above, and I wondered if she was watching us. "How big do you think it is?" my son asked.

"I don't know," I said. "Twenty feet long maybe? As long as the house. If it even was a real lake monster."

"Don't you think it's real?" Jesse asked.

"It was something, but was it a lake monster?" I said. "What would it eat? There aren't any fish in the lake."

The boy thought about this. "I think it's real," he said to me. "It could eat people." He was only eight.

Natalia seemed in a better mood after her mocha. She sat, still in her robe, at the kitchen table with a stack of magazines beside her. She was flipping through one, scissors in hand.

"A project?" I asked her.

"Making a hat poem." I saw she had several words already clipped out: *panpipe*, *Sigurd*, *Eden*, and *penetrating*. Art was her subject. "How it works," she explained, knowing I'd ask, "is you select a bunch of different words, put them in a hat, and then pull them out, blindly of course, to make a poem. The trick," she said, snipping around the word *fido*, "is not to think too much about what words you're cutting out. And to get way more than you need. You really only use about fifteen or so words to make the poem— enough to fill a pretty piece of construction paper— but you want three times that amount in the hat, for the sake of possibility."

"What color paper will you glue them to?"

"Purple. I was thinking purple."

Jesse asked, "Can I make one too?"

"Of course," she said, and they set about mangling the old magazines with their cutting, putting them to good use. Better that they collect words from magazines than even consider approaching my dictionaries. I had more than thirty locked behind a glass cabinet in my den, ordered by publication date. The oldest was printed in 1785. It was one of several of my early editions by the lexicographer Dr. Samuel Johnson. Were I to have looked through the books, arranged by date as they were on the shelves, I'd have seen the slow decay of words, their mutations in spelling, sound, and meaning. I had often read that language evolves, but the way I saw it, language seemed to pass on, slowly dying, slowly replaced with a new tongue that though it appeared to be a relative of the original, was but an analogue that arose from discordant clays, primal tongues wielding words with ignorance. I had the books to support this view, books that catalogued ancient English, books written in Old and Middle English, languages that had evaporated and been replaced, the latter replacing the former, the former replacing earlier Germanic tongues. It is really just scribbles on paper, truncated scraps of antiquity that serve as the memory of these dead languages. They do not, as some have written, survive in the form of our speech.

Yet I revered these books, these archaic words. Their forms, their origins, all of it I loved. I hoped, too, to pass this passion on to my son. He preferred his mother's books. She taught art, after all, to grade school children. I taught linguistics at the university in the next town, some twenty minutes drive away. We'd been married ten years. We had made each other's acquaintance and kept cordial company for many months before I realized she was smitten with me. How young Natalia was. I felt like an ancient tome with my grizzled beard and my thin, peppery hair when next to her, a slender book of modern poetry. It was a kindness, I think, for her to marry me, an erudite man twelve years her senior, when she could have had a younger man. The maxim goes: *There's plenty of fish in the sea.* But then again, what does love care for a fish in open water when there is one in the net?

While they created their pastiche poems, I went looking for a book that held a chapter on Dardic elision. I thought it might be useful in my own studies. I had been searching on and off that summer for the slim volume, which I remembered as having either a red or brown cover. It did not help that I could remember neither the title nor the name of its author, only that I had read some pages of it years ago and thought perhaps it would reveal a passage that I could quote for the book I was working on. I had exhausted the library's volumes, so I searched the shelves mounted on the walls in the spare bedrooms and soon began searching those bookcases and little tables that were pushed against the walls or were placed in the nooks and corners of the hallways. I had scanned those areas before, though never methodically. I wasn't a methodical man—I never stacked my papers into organized piles, I never stuck to the reading schedules listed in my syllabi, and I was not able to search those shelves in any way but a nonsensical way either.

An idea struck, and I headed to the basement, which was accessible from the garage through a white door with green trim and a wobbly brass doorknob. The basement was one open room and a partial wall of unfinished design. There was a single window; a slim light filtered weakly through the dirty pane. The man who built the basement and added a garage to the house had been a brilliant architect. He had bought the building and summered by the lake. However, these were not relaxing days for him. He was paranoid and always editing the house to match his madness. There were things in our home—little hatches, escape holes, and narrow passages. There were false walls between the bedrooms. Every way in had a second way out. The architect originally intended to rusticate his life along this new lakeshore, but whatever demons he sought refuge from—it was not known to us what haunted him so—followed him from the busy city and kept him company. We only knew that he sought solace in the act of making a maze of his shelter, an act that ended when his family finally had him locked away.

A dim and cool place, we used the basement to store the Christmas tree, holiday decorations, disused furniture, and our wine, the bottles sitting on an alveolate shelf. Near the wine was an old credenza that had belonged to my father. I flipped the light switch on, and two overhead fluorescents—one of which kept a ballasted hum—illuminated the space, and I opened the cabinet doors on the bottom portion of the antique heirloom. There were board games and books both stored there. I picked up a book with a dull red cover. There was no printing on the outside, meaning it was an old book sans its dust jacket, and I flipped through it to find the title and author. It was one of my books on language, though I wasn't sure it was the one I was looking for. I glanced at chapter titles and turned to those that sounded promising, and as I leafed through the book, something slid out of the pages and onto my lap. I picked it up. It was a photograph I had used as a pleasant bookmark. In it was captured a soft-focus image of Natalia. She had long hair the living color of primrose yellow. It was taken at a park near her parents' place when she was only a few months pregnant with Jesse. She wore a mauve shirt and a brown skirt. The backside of a big red slide towered in the background like a ladder into the sky. The book held nothing but Brythonic conjectures, and I put the book back and took the photo with me.

I thought about bringing a bottle of wine too, but there was no cause for celebration. I shut the door and went to the library where, on a low shelf, stood framed photographs of our family. I set the photo of my wife upright, leaning against a framed photograph of the three of us, me in tweed, laughing and unprepared for the snap of a camera, Jesse with his wavy brown hair and sporting a big forced grin, and Natalia wearing a blue bandana, smiling in a thin-lipped way, squinting her eyes. Around us were the golds, reds, and browns of those beautiful, dead autumn leaves fallen to the earth, shed in anticipation of that bitter cold in which animals fill out their winter coats in their own prognostic, yet opposite, reaction to the creeping tendrils of frost that culminate in the coming snow. I smiled at the photographs there and hurried back to my wife and son, giving up again the search for the vanished book.

They hung their hat poems on the refrigerator, using magnets that looked like large ladybugs and little yellow flowers. The poems: random nonsensical lines. Yet art, so ordered with the background color, the words, and their spacing selected by the artist. I asked myself: Is this chaos truly so or do those strings of words serve as a small illustration or an inevitable reflection of a panlogistic hand that set the earth to spinning, that told the trees to let go their leaves and the birds to fly and the bears to sleep? There was so much that I wished to convey to that possibility of creative intelligence, but what orisons could an agnostic give, and what good would it do anyway if all things were ordered in the precision of a grand and unfolding act and to live was simply to be a brad stuck in the woodwork of creation?

Like all days, the sun climbed, meals were cooked and consumed, and the sun began to sink into the horizon as we ate our supper.

"I had thought about wine with our meal but decided against it."

"Why?" Natalia asked, adding butter to her steamed asparagus.

"There is nothing to celebrate."

"Robert." She looked at me with an incredulous arch of her eyebrows.

"There's not."

"Of course there is," she said, and as a pronouncement declared: "We can celebrate the discovery of a lake monster."

"Are you sure?" I asked.

"Yes. Yes, I am. I'd love some wine."

Our son asked, "Can I have some chocolate milk? To celebrate?"

I held her as she cried, curled on the bed, an empty wine glass next to her. Swoops of the overhead dark sunk its teeth into the wine-colored leavings of the day, eating the last life of light and darkening the rectangle of our bedroom window. She was riddled with cancer. The doctor had told us the day before. There'd be no remission this time. She wailed, "How to tell our son?" He was to face more than morbidity, but loss.

"Do not number my days." She had cut the man off before he could say more.

"There would be little point," the doctor had said in return. "In my experience, when it is this progressed and surely terminal, you'll know the tide when it reaches the shore."

With the first treatment we had been cagey and researched our options before taking any pills to shrink the tumors or subjecting her to radiations. We chose an experimental treatment, shown to be prophylactic in initial trials. We were hopeful. Then the cancer did wane, and she grew healthy. It was a blow when it came back. We continued the treatment and combined it with radiation therapy. Her hospital nights were sleepless and filled with pain. Her hair, all of it—from her blond locks to the fine down that graced her toes—fell out. Our son cried to see his mother wasted so. He thought she was dying and did not understand how this woman, hairless and hollowed of her fat, could be getting better. Even he, a child, recognized how ill a creature she was.

The treatments done, the cancer killed, she returned home, and Jesse watched day after day—I saw him studying her—as she regained health and hair, and she became stronger. Her hair grew in slow and brown, and she returned to work, to her arts and crafts, her finger paints and papier-mâché pigs, instilling skill and design into the already creative capacities of her schoolchildren.

"I want to tell him myself," she murmured. I stroked her hair. She was too drunk to open her eyes.

"Okay," I said. What floodgate did we unlatch when we let the doctors cut out that cancerous tumor tucked in her ovaries, a teardrop-shaped thing of bloodied veins so like a malformed neonate eliminated from an inamorata of my younger years? The first treatment we chose, in part, to save her fertility. The second treatment—when the cancer began to grow again—destroyed all hope of another child for us. Now where did that new mutation come from? What awful thing sprung up from the grave of her irradiated eggs and swam through her blood, multiplying and implanting itself throughout the width and breadth of her body? It is such a cruel Logos that dictates the universe should be so balanced in destruction and creation. Even the lithosphere sinks back into the molten faults as the mountains rise. Give me one, for both is too much to bear.

I drove home from my office on campus, a place I had not yet searched for my book. I had not found it. There were, however, other volumes I brought back with me in a box. I did not see my son inside the house. I found Natalia reading in a chair next to the window. "What did he say?" I questioned.

"He asked if I was going to have to go back to the hospital."

"Oh."

"He looked relieved when I told him no," she said, a sad half-smile on her face.

"Do you think he gets it?"

She chuckled and shook her head. "Come on," she said, stretching and asking me to assist her out of the seat. "Help me make lunch."

My son became obsessed with the New Bedford Lake monster. They nicknamed it Billy. A skeptical journalist for the paper called it that in jest, but the name caught on and stuck, and there were even handmade clay figurines of Billy—or how he might look—for sale in the local gift shop, so I bought one for Jesse, which he kept on a nightstand next to his bedside. Every game with his friends came to involve the lake monster. They took turns being the serpent, and sometimes they all played the part of the monster, as if the lake could hold a plethora of such mythic beasts. Natalia brought out crayons for him to draw Billy, and in my son's imagination, the lake monster became an aquatic firedrake, sticking his neck out of the water and blowing an orange ball of flames into the sky. When a lone boater disappeared from his boat, Billy was quickly blamed, although I thought a more likely suspect to be the near-empty box of beer found on the craft. The lake was dredged, no body found.

Of course, I did not believe in any lake-dwelling, man-devouring cachalot, though ours was one of the new lakes, young by standards of a man's life and certainly no more than a blastula when measured by geologic time's yardstick. The water projects had been funded by the government: new lakes, rerouted rivers, dams, and other waterways across the country to keep the water fresh and flowing. There were empty reservoirs, beds still littered with the bones of fish. The world baked, the dormant grasses died, and in some places nothing grew for lack of water. So we put the water where we could and pooled it like wealth.

Not long before the waves of drought began, there were floods in the northern plains. This I had read about many years before as a student in an undergraduate biology course. People who lived in those regions would speak of an insect called, colloquially, a mosquito-eater. It was itself a mosquito, though a large one that ate other mosquitoes. No biologist had ever seen one; thus, it was a myth passed down from the times when the Missouri still wandered freely and the unschooled settlers sought explanations for what they saw, and what they saw was, perhaps, nothing more than the couplings of those dimorphic insects. But, during the floods of that year, when the river roamed again and turned the long-dry floodplains quaggy, there arose a new mosquito that fed not on the warm-blooded creatures that lived along the river; rather, it predaceously cannibalized those dipterous files of the same hematophagous family. Scientists were amazed at their discovery and published articles in rarefied journals on the newly discovered species. Those who were of the area merely reflected that they had always been aware of these carnivorous mosquitoes that ate other mosquitoes, even if the knowledge had come from a collective memory, orally transmitted over generations. These insectivores had come from eggs lain dormant in the ground for decades, waiting for a deluge to soak them to the core. Once transfused with this catalyst, there began again the beating of life within that would become the swimming larval forms, unaware of the length of their dormancy but patiently awaiting that natural act of metamorphosis, which would lead to their being caught by man again in their acts of flying, killing, and consuming after decades of wispish rumor.

If this was all true, could not, then, the lake monster likewise have been the spawn of an egg laid long ago, never having had the chance—due to some drought or dreadful quake that emptied an ancient lake—to hatch this Cretaceous, or perhaps even earlier, life-form? While not probable, it was possible, I admitted; although, how long could such an anachronism live in an otherwise lifeless lake?

My son spent unusual amounts of time outside that summer. The allure of the New Bedford Lake outweighed that of movies and indoor games. Even at breakfast, he'd look out the window and the question would form on his siruped tongue before his last bite of pancake was downed, and there was little purpose in denying him, the Argus of the lake, permission to play outside. He would play on that liminal shore of childhood where phantasms undulate on the surface of reality and the fetters of fact are brittle and abandoned, cast aside to rust in the elements and become no more substantial than the friable shellstone of other dead and forgotten things, of a time with other rules and realities, which also held no potency or authority any longer. While Jesse spent hours at his imaginative task, I could not sit long at my writing desk, and before I knew it, I'd find myself in the kitchen, in the library, or opening a secret passage in the wall and peering into the dark, creaking innards of my house. "Write," she said. "Go and research your elided words, babe. I want you to do what you normally do. Both of you."

"I never stay put at my desk," I protested.
"But your page is never blank."

They sat outside on lawn chairs while I grilled.
The fire danced on the black charcoal, dripping
grease from the meat into the flames, making an
inconstant sizzle. The clouds were thin in the sky,
and through them the sun fell in shaftlike yellows.
We thought they were clouds of dust from the
empty fields of abandoned western farmland,
though we were not sure. Still, the sunsets had been
spectacular that week, casting our evening world in a
ruby glow that deepened to a velvety crimson as the
sun sank away. Natalia sipped iced tea and wore
large sunglasses, which many men would have
found beautiful—a svelte woman with shades,
reclining against the backdrop of a lake fired in
yellow tints, the mellow calls and cries of doves
amplified across the water's surface so that she, the
woman, seemed a symbol of the physical self, self-
aware and at ease in the reified concept of nature:
earth, wind, and water, spaces that could seem so
measured by the continuity that codified the day
into ephemeral intervals of computer and work and
couch crashing until it seemed weeks since the body
and mind had been able to be engrossed in all that
the sun touched—yet I considered the dark lenses
of her glasses a rasure of her beauty, for her eyes
were that which I loved best, those unchanging rings
of amber that time could not wrinkle or mar for as

long as she took in breath. But it must be remembered that the lake there was dead, and the girl, for all her beauty, was a mess of nature's inharmonious imperfections, and the sky itself was inundated with the dust of cadaverous soils.

She turned her head toward me. Where had her eyes been resting before? From where she sat, it could not have been the shore of the lake. The water was what my son's eyes studied. I, of course, watched her and my fire. Perhaps she gazed at the blue-gray smoke floating into the sky and wondered at its diffusion. Natalia had not chosen cremation, instead, she had opted for the earth, a choice that felt cyclical and held, as Hamlet pointed out, the possibility for a beggar to consume his former king. I said: Let me burn; let me burn and be done with reincarnation. Let me retire from samsara's comic misery, and let not the nutriment of my being feed that which lives and propagates life. Stop me up in a jar, an heirloom defiant till the world's shaky end.

I sent our son inside for the veggie burgers. Natalia had not eaten meat since I had known her. She said, "My parents are coming up at the end of the month. I almost forgot to tell you."

"I was wondering if they were going to visit soon."

"Sorry I didn't mention it earlier."

"That's fine," I said.

"I'm not feeling very good. I've got this massive headache, and these sunglasses are not helping."

"Anything I can do?"

"I think I'll go lie down."

"Are you sure?"

"Yeah. Come get me when you're done. Thanks."

Mother and son walked by each other. "Mom's not feeling well," I said and regretted saying it.

"Is she okay?"

"Yes," I said, "just a headache."

He sat down in his chair. "Where is her cancer at?" he asked.

"A lot of places. Throughout her body."

"In her head too?"

"Yes."

"Is it making her sick?"

"Yes."

"Is it giving Mom a headache?"

"I don't know. Could be."

"Are we going to have to take her to the hospital?"

"No. Not for the cancer and not for a headache."

"Good." He smiled.

The frozen veggie burgers cooked fast. I had it timed so the beef and the soy would finish cooking together. Jesse opened a can of soda to go with his meal, and he slurped the first spurt of foam that bubbled from the opening. The wind took the smoke across the yard. Jesse burped and then he asked, "Will you marry someone else when Mom dies?"

"I doubt it." I felt myself aged and could not fathom again finding another. Yet I had before felt the same about rekindling the fires of the heart once the flames had been snuffed and hadn't imagined I'd marry at all after the loss from that time so remote, it seemed there on the edge of the lake, a lake geographically distant and that had not existed then any more than the dream of my child asking me such a question as to make my heart sick.

There were other people who came down to the lake, crossing through the empty lot beside our house and lawn. It made me worry for Jesse, who spent his hours playing there by the water. There were far more visitors than I had ever seen before, and I wondered what kind of people came to sightsee, looking for Billy the Lake Monster. I assumed most were searching for a little fun, but what if there was a lunatic—one who would turn the tragedy of a drowned boy into evidence for the elusive inhabitant of these waters? Of my concerns my wife said, "There are worse things than madmen out there. We can't let ourselves worry over something so unlikely, Robert."

"But if it did happen?"

"A crazy person intruding in on us?"

"A lunatic murdering our son. Or you or me."

"Robert, please. If anything, this will blow over and our buddy, Billy, will fall into one of your annals of obscurity."

"Can't we be careful until it blows over?"

"How much more careful can we be than to teach our son how to handle himself with strangers? What would you do if we lived in a big city where there really are lunatics—lots of them?"

"I'm sorry. You're right."

"Of course I'm right. Now kiss me, and let's not talk about it anymore."

Still, I'd seen faces thin and fat, strangers of unknown pedigree and volition on the edge of our lawn, looking into the water in wonder, contemplation, and even hope. And I hoped that our son would listen to our admonishments and not break that line of polite wariness due to a feeling of kinship in their mutual interest in watching the water ripple, without fish though not without murk and mask. I even saw a man and a woman on a boat. The man had a stick, and he dipped it into the water like a giant ruler, and he pulled it out, and I thought I saw the woman write something on a clipboard. I could only guess what sort of baseless, pseudoscientific nonsense they were attending to. Even while grilling there in my yard, I was forced to wave at a grinning fat man in a red T-shirt who hobbled through the unkempt grass. My son saw the look of suspicion that crossed my face, and I knew I appeared the weirder for my cold civility, but it could not be helped, just as I could not pinpoint the true derivation from which arose the many branches of my pessimism toward the world.

"What is Heaven like, Dad?"

Thoughts twisted through my son's brain, trying to wrap around concepts of eternity—how I felt for the child, as well as for myself. Like so many concepts, such an abstraction cannot stand alone in being understood—if it can be understood at all—for it relies on a reference point of temporality to examine the extremes of this totality, which are but a binary opposition that no living being, I would say, can truly grasp in the web of their thoughts but can build images and associations to comfort or, perhaps, to terrify; either set of images and associations only serving as explanatory imaginings, for the truth of the matter is that annihilation and perpetuity are both beyond the reality of a living being. I sighed and answered, "No one really knows."

"Alejandro says there're streets of gold, and everybody gets a mansion."

"That is what some people think. It's a nice idea."

"But Tim says you just sing in God's light all day?" I could see Jesse's mind picturing a celestial reading lamp or chandelier, perhaps even a classroom of souls seated in desks with a golden light shining from the ceiling above, powered by everlasting love.

"People have different beliefs and opinions on Heaven, on the afterlife. They're all valid, and it's okay for people to think different things about it. The truth is that no living person knows for certain, but we should respect each opinion."

"What do *we* believe?" he asked, of course, meaning our family.

He was looking for guidance, my child; could my words lead him to a simple answer, an answer that he may have needed just then? This was a realm better suited to his mother who was practiced in answering the questions of children. Should I have said, "We believe you go to Heaven and it's a good place," and leave it at that, an easy answer to provide solace for the child? It was a falsehood perhaps no worse than sharing stories of Santa who flew through the sky in a sleigh pulled by magical reindeer across the earth to dispense presents with no reciprocation or the stork that brought babies all bundled in swaddling clothes straight to the homes of expectant parents; yet I had a need to instill the values that Natalia and I held. Ready or not here I come to introduce my son to the oubliette of uncertainty. "We believe that everyone needs to find their own answer."

We took our food inside, and my wife ate, despite her headache, and the rest of the day went well till night when, in the library, Natalia and I placed our bookmarks between pages, and we made our way to our bedroom and shed our raiment as though we had all the joys of the world cupped in our hands, and we freely poured them into each other's mouths.

2

The whispers were bruited about and the flowers were brought in by the vase. Throughout the week, visitors knocked with one hand on our lavender door while holding their vessels of flora in the other. Some were all smiles, artificers of genial discourse, and we sat them in chairs and entertained them. These friends and coworkers often brought wine and their spouses, and we sipped the intoxicating red until the sun gave way to the lesser lights of night that hung above our heads like glimmers of hope that sparked with twinkling vibrancy. The words of these smiling Dionysiacs, though they promised no peradventure of the ticking clock or its midnight outcome, conveyed the thought that life would be indulged and enjoyed while the pulse maintained the blood's fiery flow. Others came into our house as sobbing shipwrecks in a dismal ocean, dragging their anchors of grief from the wreckage of their capsized bulks up onto the sharp, froth-strewn stones. Their teary faces permitted us—especially my wife—our own tears. We entertained these guests in chairs too, but for all our attempts at joviality, the nights ended in hugs, wet cheek to wet cheek, and choked promises that our friends would be there for us should we need them, promises given and tossed in with other such words where they corraded like so many jugs of wine and whiskey tossed at the beach and spit back out as sincerely cherished and useless sea glass.

Some of the bouquets came with cards attached to them on which were written that the giver was thinking of us, or the cards were simply signed *With love*. My colleagues gave cards where they penned pithy quotes from prosateurs and poets. One stood out—a quote from Alfred, Lord Tennyson—for its strangely possessive insistence: "Dear heavenly friend that canst not die, / Mine, mine, for ever, ever mine." It is doubtful that the giver of the poem had intended possessiveness when choosing that quote; rather, I thought, those lines were saying that eternity exists not in the continuation of the soul but in the other as a memory, and by being loved *in memoriam*, one did continue to exist—all Heaven encompassed in the furrowed brain—and one's soul was no more and no less than a thought and, as each person was remembered and that person remembered had had in memory the souls that before him or her had gone, so our species was immortal down to our Adam and our Eve.

Natalia detached the cards from their bouquets and dropped them in a shoebox that contained other correspondence dating as far back as her high school days. It did not take long before the old letters were covered by these white, red, pink, and violet cards. When looking into that box, one could not tell that anything but those slips of sorrow were contained there, for the printed announcements of empathy—though each little, en masse large—shrouded all letters of life that came before.

She set the vases of flowers on tables and desks and shelves until there was little space left. Since it looked as though too many vases were clumped together in the same area, she took the flowers and tossed those that she could not save and cut the stems to size of those she could, and she tied them with string, and, in the basement, along the rafters, she strung up a length of wire and around it, looped the excess string, and hung the flowers bloom side down, dying in reverse of the way they lived, preserved in the dark, cool space above our heads. As I moved the ladder aside, one day, searching again for that vanished book, I looked up and wondered would I or Jesse someday cut down those little mummies or would they stay bound and bunched, left to rest, only to be looked upon now and then like the decorated sarcophagi in a mausoleum.

I returned from the campus library empty-handed. Inside, lamplight cut the walls with angles of yellow, and the stairs I climbed creaked in a hollow fashion that told of spaces underneath. The sound stretched to the edges of the house, rumbling through the bones of its marrowless architecture. Always these sounds were disorienting, the source of movement indiscernible and out of time, much

like a wall of rock catching the echo's echo and
painting the sloping forestland before it with the
rumbles of a distant waterfall. The navigational
method of the house was to follow voices, which—
unlike the steps and stomps and pulling and pushing
of furniture—with practice could be followed with
diligence and turning of face, like tracing a long and
fragile thread of spiderweb by sighting it just right in
the sunlight. And so I did follow the sound of their
voices, first Natalia's—soft and low like wind
through the bare limbs of a winter elm—and then
Jesse's, which twittered like a cardinal's zigzag song.
I approached without word, and they did not know
I was there next to Jesse's bedroom where he was
wrapped in a bedsheet and comforter with Natalia
by his side, talking. I caught the quiet sentence, "It is
a place of peace." So she chose as best she could to
shield him from the cutting razor of uncertainty
about the unknown that sliced her so, for I knew my
wife did not believe those words that she spread
over Jesse as a blanket against the cold truth that the
darkness of the grave terrified her.

And the emptiness of life without her—indeed,
that terrified me.

With a clearing of my throat, I made myself
known, and I stepped into the bedroom and
introduced no alteration, added nothing to what my
child's mother had said. How I envied her power to
say the right words, whereas I could only tear words
apart for meaning and weight, lay them out like

cadavers, measuring their displayed parts with analytical skill in my sterile, semiotic vacuum. Such tendresse I felt then for her in how she tethered the heart of a sentence with simplicity and supplied the full force of it not with science but with pure human compassion. We ruffled our son's hair, smacked his cheek with our kisses, and then turned off his light and shut his door. On the stair landing I took her by the wrists and proclaimed my love, and I ran us outside where the trees stood like breathless specters and the lake sank void like another sky inserted impossibly into the earth, and I kissed her and kissed her, and we made our love known to the night where above us the stars guttered like candles in the winds of that celestial black.

In the morning I wrote and referenced sources along the way and marked the passages I quoted with little sticky notes in loud limes and vibrant pinks so I could easily check them when revising. The fog was thick, and out there were deer—eating the plantlets that grew up from the ground—fading in and out of view, heads visible without bodies, bodies visible without heads, tails striding into the mist. There was no telling how many there were, for they were transitory and transfinite like the fog itself, rolling and shifting without true measure, not by scale or noosphere, in that when the fog burned off so would the deer; only recollection and writing could save those beings from obliteration, as if they would care about being saved like angels—bound in the writings of holy books—when it is humankind who truly longs to be saved and bound into that which is written with the promise of eternity; nevertheless, it is the marking down of immortal creatures that gives man and woman in the here and now a sense of hope for continuation beyond our breathing days.

A chair creaked, and I heard the pat of feet landing on the floor. The shuffled sound of locomotion belonged to Jesse who was up early as well, probably playing some silent game—hand-held technology or one borne from imagination held in his head.

The door to the den opened. The heavy wood, quiet in its swing, stirred the air in the wake of its movement. I felt the cool breeze of it brush the skin of my neck like a presence unwilling to brook my solitude. "Dad." Jesse peeked his head into the room.

"Good morning, Jesse." I turned in my chair to greet him.

"Morning. It's foggy out," he said.

"Come here." I beckoned, and he walked in. I lifted him onto my lap so he could watch the deer fragmenting in the fog like a ghost herd of the south wind, set upon the world of man in that turbulent time of morning's triumphant clash with night so that the herd may graze in the shroud of nature's earthbound war smoke and then be gone in the bright of day. But to where?

"Can they see?"

"Yes, they can."

"They must have special eyes."

"No, they don't. When you're in the fog, you can only see what's directly around you. Is there fog right in front of the window?"

"No."

"Ah, but if the deer were to look over here, they'd see fog hiding our window from view. To us, they are standing in the fog. To them, the fog is all around, though not where they are. The thicker the fog, the less far you can see. It's like being in the heavens. It's a cloud on earth."

Jesse looked at me, tilting his head in thought, like his mother.

"Don't believe me? I've been in clouds before."

"Uh-uh."

"Uh-huh. In a plane," I said. "That's the thickest vapor. You can't get that kind of condensation so close to earth."

"I want to go in a cloud."

"Do you want to play in the fog?"

"Yeah."

"Go ahead. But stay in our yard. Don't go too close to the water, please."

"Why?" he asked.

"Because there are wet rocks you can slip on and because it's foggy and because I said so."

"Okay."

He skipped away, and I continued to watch out the window, and the deer continued to recede with the fog, their distinct parts—hooves to heads—less visible and less detailed, but their bodies began to appear as fading silhouettes. They were gone by the time Jesse went outside, although the fog was still there, and perhaps the deer were still hiding in the thicker fog that lingered beyond the line of our property, though if they were, they could not be seen. Jesse appeared in view of my window. He had dressed himself in sneakers, blue jeans, and a green jacket. He waved to me, and I waved back. He walked farther, and a wisp of fog caught him and blurred him in my vision. My heart leaped, and I had to breathe in deep and slow; I had to remember he would be fine, that to him there was no fog, no anything enshrouding him. Then he ran off, out of view, toward the backyard, trying to chase the fog, trying to lose himself in that simulacrum of angel's bedding.

As the fog cleared, there arose something red and of such a vivid and pure solid color, contrasting with the translucent grays and hazy images, that it seemed to be a melancholic hallucination, too real to be real, a thing of geometry and color floating in the air with no operant mechanism to explain its appearance to me. Then, slowly, the base of the red was revealed, at first as a simple dark streak like a shadow through the fog and, within minutes, it grew into the same red as its upper part. The top part began to grow downward as the bottom part climbed upward, until the two halves met and made the whole of the object plain. It was a tent, pitched out in the land next to ours.

I watched the tent awhile, all the fog having vanished with the force of the morning light, as though a congregation of nocturnal ghosts dissipated, their right to the sun forfeited in exchange for an eternity of nights. The tent was still, and no slumberer stretched or stirred to leave the confines of that waterproof fabric pegged in the ground, as though this was some vacationland, which it was not, and whoever it was in the tent would have to piss directly onto the earth, there being no facilities, and breakfast, I assumed, would be cold or skipped entirely, there being no firepit, and I wondered how long this person would stay inside the tent or if he or she had risen early to fish in the lake, where there were no fish or, more likely, to look in the barely lit waters for a sign of the lake monster. Though sleeping in or simply lying in that red tent is what I would have done if it were me, wrapped snug in a sleeping bag, listening to the mezzo piano notes of the first birds to open their dewy beaks and break into song, which would rise and rise into an operatic fugue as each new voice joined the chorus and sang: "Yes this is life and this is death and these are the worms we slip down our gullets and these are the songs we sing to our mates and these are the cries of pain and squawks of fear and the work songs we whistle while we build our nests and this, this here is the shout of the glory of flight as we catch the air beneath our wings, and, knowing the secret of all winged creatures, we sing with open throats that yes, it's true, the world is smaller the higher you fly."

At last I let my gaze drop back to my books, which looked smeared with words, lists and lists of words, and I could hang onto none of them and could not remember where I wanted the rest of the unfinished sentence I was working on to go. A clock struck, a note rang out to claim the passing of an hour, and the house above creaked, indicating that my wife was taking her first morning steps.

She appeared in my study and said, "Couldn't sleep?"

"But I did write. Quite a bit."

"That's good," she said. She stood in thought. "I'm thinking of baking cookies for tomorrow."

"Sounds good," I replied.

"Chocolate chip. My dad's favorite."

"There's a tent out there."

"Really?" she asked and came and looked out the window. She put her fists to her forehead and said, "They were probably there all last night."

"Yes," I said, and then added, "in the tent."

"Still," she said, "we were right out there. They could at least have heard us if not seen us."

"If they were awake, I suppose."

"Oh my God," Natalia said and walked into the kitchen, and I heard her swing open a cupboard, followed by sounds of her preparing coffee. I winced, hearing the clank of a spoon in a bowl and the angry pouring of cereal. I pretended to write, and she did not ask if I had eaten. Natalia finished her food quickly and was still waiting for her coffee to finish brewing. She came back and said to me, "If you're up early, could you please make the coffee."

"Of course I can," I said. "I'm sorry I didn't think of it." I sat with her when the coffee was done and, with a measure of guilt, drank a cup.

I wrestled my unfinished sentence into the shape of an idea that I hoped might hold under the scrutiny of a scholarly eye. There was so much left to write. Where had the time gone? Had it drifted like summer's heat out over the ocean and up, even farther, past the atmosphere, and into the unreachable spaces where nothing but the residue of alpha's violent and ballooning beginning floats with no sentient thought to quantify it? And, beyond that, is it pulled, finally, into the mouth of omega, that infinitesimal puncture on the surface of God's perfect canvas where all creations' paint will eventually drain? All my time I would give to her, but as an artist, she required time and space to engage in the act of creation, and so she spent a cantle of hours on her projects, which ranged from mature to childish, and, really, it did not matter to her what she was creating as long as it was an act of expression, and it did not matter to me the quality of her art as long as it came from the imaginative depths of herself. She forced me, also, to my desk, and I knew that I had to continue to write and work on my book.

Natalia did insist we both work but never made demands for a quotidian sense of normalcy; with so many flowers and visitors who brought them, her cancer was hardly the elephant in the room, for who could ignore the subject—not that we'd stick it in a corner or drawer if we were able, wishing it'd stay put; rather, we let it linger here and there in a casual way, which we hoped would be healthy for Jesse and for us. After all, we had practice with cancer and contemplating death; only this time, the end was placed ahead of her on the road of life, with no mile markers for us to measure the distance made toward it. Yet we knew the endpoint was looming; the doctor soothsaid the printing of her name on the reaper's necrology, which he was given prepublication to fact-check, running his skeletal finger across the manuscript and scanning the names with his empty eye sockets, nodding his head in assurance that the list was sound and, as soon as the second hit when Atropos sheared through that bundle of strings, he'd send off the paper to its eventual publisher and take up his sickle to collect the souls that waited shivering in the frosty winds of death.

The sentence done, I looked through the window and saw the tent in motion, moving like vibratile gelatin. I watched it thrash, and then out crawled a young man followed by a young woman. Both wore jackets in the cool morning air. The boy helped the girl up, and they kissed, their fingers intertwined. She talked. He listened. They smiled. I wondered what they were saying and why they had chosen to tent out there. Then I saw her nails—long and painted cherry red—as she touched his shoulder. This prompted me to look more closely at her face. I studied the smile, her large white teeth, the shape of her nose, the color of her hair. I could not be sure, yet it looked like the girl from the video that I had seen first and that Jesse had played over and over, not to see the girl but to watch the thing in the lake that surfaced behind her.

I could write no more, so I ventured to the kitchen to wash some plates and pans that sat in the sink. I plugged the drain with the stopper and ran the water hot and from a bottle squeezed a line of blue dish soap, which sat at the bottom of the sink for some seconds until I put my hand into the water and stirred the liquid. I watched as the suds began to cover the surface, churned by the water streaming down from the faucet.

The pans I did last because they had been used the day before to fry morning eggs, caramelize onions, and brown our buttery pancakes, leaving a smeary grease. I took a scouring pad to the cast-iron kitchenware, and the water went dark, and the matter I lifted stuck to my hands, got caught in the lifelines of my palms.

I was drying the dishes when Natalia—dressed in a red shirt with frilled sleeves and denim capris—returned.

"The couple outside," I said.

"Who?"

"In the tent."

"A couple?" she said, folding her arms.

"Yes. A boy and a girl. I think I recognize them. Or at least her."

"A student of yours? Oh, that's wonderful."

"No," I said. "From the lake monster footage. I think that's her."

"Well," Natalia yawned, "I suppose they're back for part two of their documentary."

I heard the door open and slam shut, followed by sounds of Jesse discarding his wet shoes. He trotted into the kitchen and asked, "What's for breakfast?"

"A second helping of fifteen minutes of fame," I replied.

"What?" he asked.

"Daddy's just trying to be silly," Natalia said. "And failing. Here, I'll get you some cereal."

"I don't want cereal. I want toast."

She looked at him and said, "Then why did you ask, 'What's for breakfast?' if you already knew what you wanted?"

"I don't know," he mumbled, looking down and playing with the zipper on his jacket.

"Well, then toast it is."

"I'll be back," I said. I went out and opened the garage door. At first I wasn't sure what I was going to do. I went to the car, drove it out of the garage, opened the trunk, and emptied it out. To myself I said this was an opportunity to organize the tools and rags and the emergency roadside kit. I told myself I was searching for my book on Dardic elision. What I was actually doing was using the car as an excuse to peek around the corner of the house, spying on the tent, trying to sight the young lady to discern if she was the girl in the video or had only a mere likeness to her. I glimpsed the young man and woman talking and holding hands. A moment later, he was halfway in the tent. With a third peek, there was no one in sight. They must have walked down to the water. I could neither see them nor did I hear their voices, even in the morning's quietude. Only their tent stood in my vision—a red alien, a structure of modernity amid the flora of my rustic scenery, impressed in a way worse than the simple treading of pilgrims in search of the surreal being they believed to be harbored in the sanctuary of the lake's brown water. The tent was anchored to that earth, and it could be that the owners of it were the same who brought the spectacle of their film into the backyard of our lives.

I pulled the car back into the garage and returned inside. Natalia had started preheating the oven, and there were cupboards open, and on the counter she had spread her bags of ingredients—flour, baking soda, sugars, chocolate chips—and also bowls and a set of matching measuring spoons. She was searching for a measuring cup, which Jesse had probably put away in the wrong drawer. "Thanks for doing the dishes," she said as I dug out the electric mixer for her.

"I'm pretty sure that's them out there," I said.

"Who?" Jesse asked.

Natalia said, "You went outside just to see?" gesturing with butter in one hand and a bottle of imitation vanilla in the other.

"No. I went to clean the car. Though I did happen to get a decent view of her while out there."

"Hum. I took a glance out the window and didn't see them. I figured they walked down to the lake."

"Who?" Jesse asked again.

"I must have seen them before they walked off. I wasn't watching them closely," I fibbed.

I turned to Jesse. He stood at my feet, his eyes pleading for an answer to his inquiries. "No one, Jesse," I answered him. I looked at Natalia. She shrugged. "Just some people. I thought maybe it was the girl from the video. The one with Billy."

"Neat," he said and ran off, his footsteps clattering to distant places in the house as he raced up the staircase, a game forming in his mind, the girl already interpolated into his fantasy. As his voice rang out in his solitary game with his new imaginary playmate, I wondered if she had ever before registered as more than a blip on the radar of his fantasyland. I doubted so, and I could not decide if she were being boxed now by his play or if her sudden presence was a further intrusion into the landscape of his creativity, just as the monster had been. I went to the window and watched, and I placed my hands on the dusty windowsill, and when I lifted them, I saw the imprint I left there. The dust I had cleared made evident the dust all around it, and I thought how there was no polish or rag that could repristinate my life, for it was more than dust and more than monsters that had settled and nested into the seams and cracks of my soul.

As my hands rested on the windowsill, they were warmed by the sun. I flexed my fingers in the light, and it felt as if the heat had moved to warm the bones contained therein. I looked and saw the grass was flamed by dew made golden with the rays of the rising sun and that much of the world had become distinct in the brightness of day. The leaves, which had been massed into one large and dark form, could be picked out in the light each individually. Little swallows could be seen swooping low to catch morning insects, also animated by the day and its warmth, as they rose into the air in pursuit of their short-lived errands and, further, the day allowed the detail hidden in the dark to be examined because in

the dark there lay pitfalls of speculation and things
incomprehensible without a torch, such as the sun,
to excite the mind to full understanding.

There were hunters in the dark and the hunted,
and one could imagine the hemisphere in darkness
and the things that might happen in the night. Then
one could envision the daybreak and what might be
found there and what could follow—aftermath and
circumspection—a dead dreamer ripped apart by
tooth and claw. This is what the day gives—a
chance to judge rightly the occurrences of the night;
the day gives heat to that. The day gives fire to the
soul, for the soul sees better in the morning, and my
soul was heated, and my soul saw clearly, and my
soul was enraged.

Yet there was a question of value to be
pondered: What is rage worth when it is life that one
is raging against? I clenched my fists in an anger that
had no locus or object on which to center, and the
anger meandered like a burning wildfire, crossing
and recrossing the burnt flesh of the temple that was
my body, and it seeped from me and spread down
through the floorboards into the crawlspaces, and
even there it ran amuck until it found a hole to
escape into the earth, and it pushed through that
godless filter with malevolent expurgation, scraping
off all impurities of love and kindness that traveled
with it until it finally reached the water as pure hot
rage, a dot of heat in the cold and lifeless dark, and I
knew it was swallowed by the beast that dwelled

there and this was energy enough for that monstrosity to hunker in that place another thousand years, should it need to.

"Robert," she called.

I went to the kitchen. "Yes?"

"The eggs," she said and squatted on the floor in front of the fridge, its door open, the bleak light paling her face, which ran with tears. "They're all rotten," she said.

I looked, and, yes, they were. All of them had rotted through the shell and stuck to the bottom of the newly opened carton.

"How are they all rotten?"

"Are they old?" I asked.

"No. No," she screamed.

"It's okay," I said. "It's okay."

"It's not. It's not okay," she cried. "How can I make cookies?"

I bent down and said gently into her ear, "I'll buy more eggs."

I calmed her, and she wiped her tears with her hands. "Hurry then," she said, "I've already started mixing things."

I tossed the carton with all the wasted eggs into the trash and went back outside. I looked over toward the tent, and they were there—the boy squatting and the girl beside him, both staring intently at something I could not see. I observed them when the thing they were watching flew over their heads, casting a momentary shadow on their faces and honking with alarm. As it flew overhead, the two turned to watch it. The cygnet flapped and then was gone, hidden in the trees. After the bird sunk into the lakeside foliage, the boy stood and faced the girl. I could hear not the words themselves that she said, but the tone of excitement came through, and I could see her investing significance in the moment, a moment of wonderment to meet so closely with nature. She was tying the young swan to herself and her man, just as lovers claim a romantic song or film as theirs and stab it with the arrow that had shot from the bow of Cupid and struck them with dumb love. They plant it there in the name of the song or film or book or what be it, and on its shaft they hoist up the flag of cheap fabric upon which is stamped the camp of their faces.

As she was talking, the boy glanced at me, turning just his head while his girlfriend chatted, and our eyes met. He smiled a knowing smile, and then he faced his girlfriend; his words hushed her, and her pale face blushed. I felt my face flush red—a different red—and, shaking, I got in the car and sped away.

I selected a carton of eighteen large brown eggs from the humming cooler at the corner gas station. The cashier ran my payment and checked the eggs before bagging them for me. I walked across the lot with the carton. The air was cool, and all was quiet there in the open world underneath the puffy white clouds where I could hear my own footfalls and the sound of grit crunching beneath my feet as I headed toward my car. As I opened the car door, the rumble of thunder growled in the distance, and I looked out at where the stentorian sound poured from, and through gaps in the trees I could see the dark blue horizon whence it came. Clutching the steering wheel, I drove home through slats of light and slats of shadow. Big white clouds sped above, pushed by an invisible pressure system of the coming storm, as if these good-natured puffs of moisture feared being swallowed by the raging thunderhead and, so, fled speedily along.

I would ask them when I returned, and I was certain they would tell me the truth: How did all the eggs there, a whole carton, go bad? Were they from the same clucking hen, laying her grade A egg shells filled with rotten yolk built upon the misaligned bonds of degraded DNA, or had some country farmer, driven to poverty by industrial farming, hex the eggs of a few unaware chickens, using the curse jotted upside down and in reverse—like a child's scribbles of pretended cursive—found in the back of a great-great-grandmother's diary? But the rain—it would come and leak through the loose ribs of the roof on the poor farmer's chicken coop while, inside the house, the farmer would look up from canning tomatoes and, seeing the rain, he'd be reminded of times when the sky let loose so much water that tractors sunk into the earth they worked. Likewise, the rain would come clattering down onto the industrial complex that housed cages stuffed with birds, and the young men who worked there, pulling the carcasses of suffocated chickens out from the ruck of living fowl, would look up at the ceiling, which drowned the place with the noise of the downpour, and they would think of their grandfathers' barnyard chickens that roamed the grounds, bound by no fence, and they would fill with an ahistoric longing for a time that did not belong to them, a time when rain did not mean the stuffiness that brought death to more birds, a time they believed was simple. The clouds can flee, the farmers young and old can dream, but the cycle remains the same in drought time or flood time; when the water does come down, it sinks into the earth, follows those secret pathways through the dirt to the greater bodies of water, and then it is taken by the sun and returned to the air where it condenses and becomes again a cloud. There is no escape. Time is always the same, and there is no true distinction between now and then. Inevitably the body will return to the earth, and rain will return to the sky. I would demand an answer. Damn the eggs—they could wait. I would know the truth, and they would tell me if they had filmed that thing in the water as they said or if it was a sham and there really was no hope that a living prehistoric thing, unknown, unnamed, and unclassified could emerge from the waters of a new and dead lake. They would tell me, yes or no, if the miracle of a stagnicolous anachronism in the lake that touched the rocks on the shore of my backyard—usurping the logic of asymmetric time—was real.

I parked the car and walked to the spot of their tenting and examined the impression left in the grasses. The shoreline was empty of any person. The sky darkled and sipped away the light, taking with it the knowledge I thought I could obtain with my blunt questions. Soon the cloak of storm would wash away this last sign of their visit, proof they'd come back with their answers and left with them still securely placed in the back of their young throats, and I wished to watch over that spot of crushed grass, as if by observance I could ascertain some secret message, but my wife was inside and waited for her eggs so she could begin her baking, and so I turned away and walked back to the car. I went in the house, the egg carton in hand, and said, "They left."

3

They arrived the next day, and it was still raining. When it first started, there fell fat drops, bloated with the dust of the air, and it rained an ocherous coating on everything, and all the world outside looked stagnant, as if years of dust had been allowed to accumulate like fallout in a vacated landscape, the world left to weather like bones. The rain calmed with the passing of the cold front, but with that cold air came an endless chain of gloomy gray clouds that followed like a sullen army dripping tears that washed the corpseland visage left in the wake of their front-line comrades. They came with wet jackets, muddy shoes, and cold hands, which gripped our own warm ones, and they hugged us. Her parents' names were Thaddeus and Cheryl. Thaddeus was tall with a big belly, but he was muscularly built from years of construction work. He was then a foreman, his time split equally between the demolition of houses and the building of them. Cheryl was short and plump. She spent a few hours four days a week in the treasury office of the city in which they resided. I carried their suitcases up to the spare bedroom and hung their wet jackets in the recently emptied closet. They slipped their shoes off at the door and nestled themselves into the chairs at the kitchen table before a plateful of chocolate chip cookies. The heater kicked on, and Natalia brewed coffee.

Jesse gobbled up his cookies and said, "Grandpa Teddy, want to see my room?" There was newly obtained paraphernalia of childhood that he wished to show his grandfather.

"In a little bit, Jesse," Thaddeus answered. "I need a refreshment after that long drive." He dipped his cookie into the coffee. Pieces broke off as he brought it to his lips, and they fell back down into his cup, splashing coffee on his blond moustache. I brought him a spoon so he could fish out the wet chunks of dough.

"Hey, I heard you have a lake monster named after you," he said.

"After me?" I asked, puzzled.

"Yeah. Bob the Sea Monster," he laughed.

"Actually, the mythological fish of the New Bedford Lake is named Billy, not Bob. If I was a William rather than a Robert, you'd be right."

"Billy…Bob, they're close," Cheryl said.

"Hey, Dad, hand me another cookie," Natalia said.

"We've got the spare bedroom all set up for you," I said.

"Is this bad weather supposed to let up?" Thaddeus asked.

"Thank you," Cheryl said, "I'm sure we'll be just fine. We're just sleeping there; it's not like we're going to stay holed up in the bedroom all day long."

"Not anytime soon," Natalia answered her dad.

"We need rain; we're in a drought."

"Everywhere needs the rain," Thaddeus said. "We're always in a drought."

"Last fall was rainy too," Natalia said.

"Too late for the crops," Cheryl said, "but not the seed."

"Anyone for some wine?" I asked.

"Later," Natalia said.

"Perhaps after supper," Cheryl added.

"I don't care for the stuff," Thaddeus said.

"That's right—I think we've got beer stowed away somewhere."

"Probably from the last time you visited. So drink it all up now 'cause you might not get another chance," Natalia said.

"Oh, please, don't talk like that," Cheryl said.

"Hey, Ma," Natalia said, and she got up and hugged her, "I didn't mean it like that."

"Then how did you mean it?"

"The beer will go bad if he doesn't drink it this visit," she answered, shaking her head.

"Why's Grandma crying?" Jesse asked. A few tears trickled around her eyes.

"How about you go play. Grandpa will come check out your room after a while."

"Billy. Bob. Oh boy," I heard Thaddeus mumble to himself with a frown. He was in his chair, facing the window, through which could be discerned a blue gloom. He turned back to the table and patted his wife's hand and then his daughter's. "This is very hard for your mother. For me too. But we're here for you. And for Jesse. We don't want to forget about Jesse. It will be hardest of all on him, and we want you to know, Robert, we're here for you and will do what we can. The rain will stop soon enough. That'll lift everyone's spirits."

The talk drizzled on, voices modulating, each taking turns to sing out in our four-part polyphony of domestic articulation, the parts crisscrossing with counterpoint like a quartet in a numbers opera. The plate of cookies was depleted, and we seemed repelled from the epicenter of that vacant china and also the table, all speckled with the crumbs of our meeting. We pushed back our chairs and laid our hands on our bellies, but this was not far enough, and we stretched our hands above our heads and yawned, and we stood and backpedaled our way to the edges of the kitchen, leaning on counters, standing against a wall of cupboards, lingering at the door, but this, too, was not sufficient distance. We were pushed beyond the kitchen and out into the halls, and we wandered into adjacent rooms and opened doors into darkness and doors into light, for it mattered not the contents of the space, and we searched for no particular object. Our heads, though, did swivel as we observed the surroundings, as if they were new and of interest, and we ambled on and out and away from one another, driven by a need to step aside and into ourselves where true contemplation could not be avoided. So, like magnets of the same charge, we were pushed apart and, though we wished to connect and empathize, all the while, we had to meander away from one another to feel the subject of death in isolation, even as we continued to call out, mingling our stories, meshing our lines of dialogue, which bounced— delayed and flattened—with the vibrato of a monastic's sonorous tones in the hollow spaces of the house through which we let our conversation weave and surface, changed by its journeys in the sacristies and undercrofts of the dark.

While Thaddeus talked, he let Jesse give a tour of his room and toys. Cheryl slowly walked by a wall lined like a gallery with the artwork of her daughter. I stepped up to shelves stuffed with books and fruitlessly let my eyes blur over their bindings. Natalia sank away into a bathroom lit by a dim nightlight. Thaddeus found himself in the dark of a pantry that smelled of the grease from a deep fat fryer we stored there, and he unwittingly slid open the false wall in the posterior of the room. He smiled sheepishly at me—blushing like a boy caught playing with his sister's dolls—as he stepped into the library where I was standing at the other end, talking to him, and it wasn't long before we were joined by our wives. His carried in wine bottles and glasses, and mine had found the beer for him, and somehow we toasted to the family; there was no cause for celebration though, when the withered arm of one of the family's limbs would break off and fall to the ground before, we felt, its due time, but had we voiced this complaint, the cloaked orchard keeper there would retort with this question: "What good is the branch which no longer flowers?" and we'd have little reply to he who tends the tree of ourselves from root to fruit. With solitary steps we unthreaded the library, lingering at the shelves and eyeing the vertical titles until, at last, enfranchised from the vastness placed between our bodies, we sat down in the chairs. Conversation continued with no slack in its flow, and things were said, some offers made: ideas suggested by Thaddeus and Cheryl that I outright rejected; the imprint of Protestantism was not something we would have Jesse brought up with.

"I think we would prefer he would continue to reside with me, if for no other reason than our latitudinarian point of view."

"We weren't thinking about religion, Robert. We were just thinking of you and Jesse and what's best for him."

"Natalia was raised Methodist, and she turned out fine," Thaddeus grumbled.

I expected Natalia to chime in, but she simply listened to both sides, examining how I felt about custody and the reasons behind my hesitations of having her parents raise him.

Later, in our bedroom, Natalia asked, "Do you really have to use such large words around my dad? It makes him feel stupid."

"What words?"

"*Latitudinal*, for one."

"I think I said *latitudinarian*."

"Whatever, just tone it down, Robert. And you don't want my parents to take care of Jesse due to their religion? I am not saying that it's not important to build the virtue of tolerance in our child, but, really, they're Methodists. Is it so exotic or unusual?"

"No," I said, "it's not that."

"Then what is it? 'Cause, you know, you pretty much offended them."

"He's my son. I want to raise him. I've no argument for it other than the one I gave them."

"Robert," Natalia said, flopping beside me on the bed where I sat, "that is a good reason. It is a better reason than the one you gave, more sound because it comes from the heart. I'm sure it would have been more appreciated than lambasting them for being Christian."

"Oh, honey, but this heart is going to be hurting. If I'm drowning in sorrow, what claim can I make as a parent? Wishing to be a father is requisite, but it's not argument enough for my continued custody after you're gone, especially when they are offering to take that responsibility."

"And does pain invalidate love?"

"Perhaps. I feel that sometimes it does."

"I don't see why it can't bring people together."

"If I'm blinded with hurt, what then?"

"If when broken, your heart cannot form an emotive argument for holding onto our son when he most needs you, then maybe your latitudinarian logic is inane."

I nodded my head in understanding. "Some sunshine would make me feel better."

There was sun, but no warmth came of it, only illumination. The sluicy runnels had run their respective courses to the lake and left, here and there, small dirty streaks where the water had flowed. I was wearied by the days holed up indoors with my in-laws and wanted out to experience a sense of space in the air, unbounded by those secretive walls. Jesse, too, seemed starved for outdoor play. After the initial excitement of his visiting grandparents, especially his beloved grandfather, he became bored of his indoor confinement, whether with a friend or by himself, despite the piles of toys hoarded up in his closet and stacked along the walls of his bedroom. Jesse's antsiness and discontent—when stemming from a desire to play outside—did not displease Natalia or myself, for we believed it a mark of raising a healthy child, one who preferred skipping and running out of doors to being a catatonic lump slouched in front of flickering screens, but the side effect of this preference for the open air during those days of rainfall was that his mood darkened, and he drew melancholic lake monsters, one picture so blue I could not tell where the scribbled markings of water were displaced by the blue form of Billy. Thaddeus himself seemed eager to step outside, and I caught him twice that week out under the eaves. So we three guys put on our jackets, leaving the women, who competed in a heated card game at the house, and went out into the cold and walked along the lake.

Jesse galloped around like a happy foal, and he picked up rocks of unusual shape or color and he called out, "Grandpa Teddy. Grandpa Teddy," and he would show his finds and set them back down, unwilling to keep the beauty of the thing locked in his room but always equally afraid that another might come along and toss the rocks—rocks that he cherished for any small oddity or uniqueness—into the drink to become lost to all eyes. These were the same broodings of his mother, who debated the merits of museums and private collectors and talked of the ownership of art as others talked of the ownership of nature because to lock a painting or sculpture behind doors was, to her, an ethical question. She believed art belonged to the public, just as Jesse believed the beautiful rocks belonged to the shore. Yet without doors to bar in a masterpiece overnight, who knew who might come in and efface a painting or steal and dump a weighty statue into the water. She fretted over these considerations.

Thaddeus walked along the rocks until the house was hidden by trees, and he turned away from the wind and bent his head low, and when he turned back, he had a cigarette wedged between his lips. "You smoke, Grandpa?" Jesse asked.

"Just don't tell Grandma. 'K, Jesse?"

"Okay," Jesse said and ran off again to kick loose a rusted paint can sunk halfway into the earth.

Thaddeus turned to me and shook his head. "The doctor said I should quit. Bad for the heart."

"And?"

"And Cheryl would kill me if she knew I still smoked, even just on occasion. Especially since Natalia's fights with cancer. She bugs me about it to this day. Says I'll get cancer too from all my years of smoking."

"I won't judge."

"I should quit."

"Yes, you should."

Thaddeus looked at me with a question in his eyes but refrained from asking. The sky was so bright and so cold. It was too cold for how hot it had been.

"I wish I had brought a fishing pole," he said.

"It wouldn't do you any good," I replied.

"Oh, yeah. No fish. I remember you mentioned that once before. What use is a lake if there's no fish in it? What's up with that anyway?"

"The New Bedford Lake is...well, new. It had fish in it once."

"What happened?"

"Oh, the county tried. Some of the first fish were sick to begin with. They should have bought from a more expensive fish farm, I guess. The diseased fish got the other fish sick. So the county attempted to fill it again. The second batch just didn't take. The project ran out of money, and no one has voiced much concern about a third attempt to stock the lake."

"It'd pay in the long run from selling fishing licenses."

"I'm sure the county had the same thought. But it's hard to create an ecosystem from scratch. Hard to build health from unhealth. Much easier to destroy that which is vital and fecund."

"Fecund?"

"Fertile," I said.

"Oh."

We walked along a little ways more to where there were less rocks jutting from the lakeshore, allowing bulrushes and cattail to grow. It wasn't much longer before we reached the property line of another house on the lake, marked by a *No Trespassing* sign, the once bright yellow words faded by time.

"At least they tried," Thaddeus said.

"Huh?" I inquired.

"To stock the lake."

"Yes."

"I'm thinking," he said, "maybe you should get a second opinion."

"About what?"

"Natalia."

I studied him, a father who loved his daughter.

The leaves on the trees waved noisily in the wind, and Jesse stood off from us, tossing dull gray rocks into the water. The rocks made a dunk sound, were swallowed, submerged. I imagined they made a cryptic pattern on the muddy lakebed, like a lover's white petals plucked from a daisy's yellow capitulum, the last one stating the outcome—the end.

"They only tried twice to stock the lake with fish. That was enough."

"But *you* could try. There's always hope, right? You can't give up because one doctor says it's too progressed."

"What do you want us to do," I said, "throw brickbats of pills and potions, of treatments and technology at it, this fortress of nascent flesh that's regrown in the woman we'd both like to save? You think we can assail this bizonal material that on high cements together the very steppingstones to Valhalla and that below the smiths use as a solvent to eat away the rocks in the deep and fiery places of the earth? Is it this, this cancer, this inscrutable substance blessed by the gods—utilized, too, by the devils underneath—that you think can be combated? Then combat it. Ha. Go on. Lift your stone from the rubble and hurl it. See what dents *you* can lay."

My troublous words fell quite unpleasantly on his ears. He exhaled the smoke in his lungs, and he said, "This is really what goes on in your head, huh?"

"You bet it is."

Jesse ran, tossed another rock. The wind whipped, took the smoke rising from the cigarette as quickly as it came out and propelled it invisibly across the lake. It seemed the sky grew brighter and bluer.

"Well, I'm sorry."

"For what?"

He shrugged. "For everything."

"You shouldn't be. Not for everything."

The days of their visit spun by. Summer was taking its leave with insouciance, trotting off without so much as a kiss of warm rays to mark its farewell.

After our talk on the banks of the cold lakeshore, Thaddeus was careful in his conversing with me, keeping all subjects mundane and material, yet these earthy words were brought into being imbued with the demiurgic blueprints of eternity, and no amount of secular talk could prescind my mind from its contemplations of the whittling knife of time, paring away the living moments until the fresh figure of her soul was formed, and that soul waiting to be found in the midst of the wood was the idea from which was based the corporeal Natalia. I could not blame Thaddeus. The things I spoke were a shock to his sensibilities, and, while he did not necessarily understand each and every word I said, the power— and if not that, then the pain—with which I spoke had riven open the seams of hope and showed it to be an empty package, devoid even of a note of explanation for its barren interior. There was simply nothing there. So, for all his *not* talking of death, each innocuous word he chose had attached to it its inimical opposite; thus, all his efforts floundered, for each word he spoke could only be another reminder that she was dying.

Cold wind snaked through the grasses, rose up to the trees, bringing everything to movement, making it restless, and giving everything noise. The west wind came after they left—Thaddeus, Natalia, and Jesse. They went out to shop and to eat. Jesse wanted ice cream, despite the dropping degrees. We could feel it. I turned the furnace up. Still the wind wailed, and we could sense it running along the outer walls of the house and skating continuously across the rooftop, and we, just like all else, were made restless by the wind.

Cheryl and I walked along the wall where Natalia's paintings hung. We paused briefly at each and then moved on. "You know," she said, "I did some painting in my time."

"Is that so? Natalia never told me."

"Third grade. Then, again, in eleventh. Art class both times. Maybe I should have encouraged her more. She was always drawing. I never saw the point. Expensive tutors and workshops run by people who couldn't get but a couple of their own works in galleries. An art village with so many failed artists. That's our little town. When she said *art major* I said at least specialize in art education."

"She said okay?"

Cheryl nodded. "She said okay. I like these clouds here. Such real textures in this little painting."

"I don't think you advised wrong. She loves kids."

"All right. Now this one with the two dogs is quite abstract."

"Ghostly," I suggested.

"Yes."

Cheryl stopped in front of a painting of a snowman with a coal smile, carrot nose, and a corncob pipe, wearing only a top hat and with three vertical buttons in the center of his coatless torso. She squinted at it.

"See the sky?" I asked.

"It's night."

"The moon and stars. The shadows play off the moon. But the red star, see that?"

"No, where? I see blue, yellow, white."

"There," I pointed.

"Okay."

"Look between the stars. It's the Milky Way. It's the heavens spilled out in the background. It could be snow if it wasn't for the black sky. Do you see it yet?"

"Oh," she exclaimed, "it's Santa and his sleigh."

"Blotting out the stars. The red star is Rudolph's nose. The extra reindeer in the lead, even though it is a clear night."

"When did she paint this?"

"She said she painted it sometime in college. Jesse liked the painting so we hung it. I think she titled it something like *Evidence of Saint Nicholas in Nighttime Photograph*."

"That title's pretentious."

"Maybe Natalia was wrestling with God."

"How so?" She turned to face me.

"Saint Nicholas. Santa Claus. A myth for children that when we grow up we no longer believe. Like the myth of any supernatural being, it lacks evidence; I take this painting to be a statement on evidence, on growing up."

"She's a good soul," Cheryl said. "She knows, inside, God will take her home. It isn't only about belief and devotion, but love and goodness. Our church believes even the good who haven't heard the good news go to Heaven."

"Is it the same for the good, unbelieving soul as it is for the devout up there?"

"Only God, the angels, and those who've gone to Heaven know for sure."

"I thought it would be explained somewhere in the Good Book."

"By faith, Robert. By faith. It's all allegory. Those who take it literally are duping themselves. We can't comprehend the afterlife, and I'm not sure we will once we get there."

"Can it be said then that it is truly unknowable?"

"Perhaps," she said. She walked to the next painting. "Or maybe there's knowledge of it planted in the heart. Maybe it can never be entirely unknown."

I put on my driving gloves and went to the car after a meeting with the head of my department. I had been granted an early sabbatical. The crisp air smelled reminiscent of a walnut grove, and I squinted in the brightness of daylight and looked out to the east where there were mountains of sheer white clouds slowly fissuring in the sky. Frantic squirrels ran across the road, and I passed joggers donned in their cold-weather running suits.

Thaddeus had said he would cook supper, and when I arrived I found everyone outside in their jackets, standing around the charcoal grill from which emitted a pleasant-smelling smoke. "Steak," he said. There were also potatoes wrapped in tinfoil, and inside the house there was a pot of vegetables steaming on the stove.

I glanced at the grill and asked my wife, "Should we start a veggie burger or something for you?"

"I'm going to have steak tonight," she said.

"Steak? You're going to eat meat?"

"Yeah," she said. "I feel like eating some steak."

Thaddeus smiled at me a smile of triumph, as if this were a sign of winning some argument. And perhaps it was one he once had with her, and he was merely gloating with his grin, wishing accolades on his trivial victory. Surely, though, he could see as I saw it too, that Natalia was letting go of that which would not matter much longer. This worried me, but she smiled, Cheryl smiled, Thaddeus smiled, and Jesse, playing close by the lake, waved and smiled, so I also smiled. Then, overhead, there flew a gaggle of geese, and we watched as they went past, honking all the way. No flock of migratory birds ever landed there at the New Bedford Lake, not even for a short stopover, nor did any ever choose these waters as their summer grounds. As more lakes dried to mere muddy pools and to dusty dents in the earth—I wondered—would these birds learn to estivate at new bodies of water or would they land again and again at the drained places of the earth, parched but for the dewfall's paltry summation?

Cheryl and Thaddeus left, luggage in hand, hugs given, and they waved at us three—their child with her husband and offspring—and in their van they began the trip back to the place where they made their keep of cushy couches, floral wallpaper, and the family photographs they framed and affixed to the walls or set copiously on whatever available surface could be found. Jesse waved until the van left his sight; then he ran off to a friend's to play.

Inside, Natalia shed her sole piece of clothing—a tent dress of pink and yellow coloring, those two hues swirling and melding together—and tossed it aside like an animal's forgotten exuviae. She stood pale and beautiful, the white daylight illuming her skin as she bent over the couch. Outside, the first unverdured leaf, wiled red by the electric incantation of the autumn air, snapped its stem and fluttered to the still-green floor below it. All the trees would follow this seasonal progression of denuding their branches of foliage and would face the winter with stoic nakedness. But if I could have, I would have held that moment forever, a moment when only one fall leaf had yet found the ground, when the light poured in shafts that enwrapped us like an incubator of renascent love, and if I could have, I would have ripped the gnomon from the face of her lifespan's dial and tossed it into the slough where it would be lost, and, afterward, no telling of the hour could anymore be made for her.

More leaves did, of course, fall, and friends came by bearing still more vases of flowers, and Natalia let them crowd out the knickknacks and treen, no longer bothering with the process of sorting, hanging, and drying these odorous bundles. Instead, she spent her time baking cookies, apple pies, and morning muffins. She cooked up meals for us, but more so for herself. Once even, she bought a tube of venison sausage, and we ate the gamey meat she had prepared; none of us had eaten anything like it before. No more did Natalia shy away from a cut of meat. She sawed and chewed and ripped into the flesh of animals farmed for their taste, and she enjoyed. Against expectations, she did not develop the cachexia that was typical of her condition; rather, she became voracious, practicing no frugality with her intake. She ate her three main meals plus elevenses, bedtime snacks, seconds at dinner, and frequently savored the flesh of two fruits with lunch. Her face filled out, her cheeks no longer sunk but became full and red when she smiled. Her bony hips and butt, her arms and legs and, yes, the ribs below her breasts were layered with fat, like an animal bulking up for the winter famine. This is not to say she was corpulent. These extra pounds enveloped her with a sense of full-bodied health, and it was a joy to look at her figure that appeared unaffected by the disease tunneling through her flesh. Who could believe that Natalia held inside her a growing and irremovable cancer? Jesse himself, although so young, saw this change in her outward appearance and sensed she radiated health, and, I believe, I observed in the innocence of his eyes an unburdening of the fear that soon his mother would leave him for a place unknown. What could he think? There were no hospital visits, her parents had left and still she had not died, and then she grew ripe like a berry—delicious and bright, full of vibrant color. I longed, though, to keep him from being deluded by this but loved him too much to illustrate how all such fruit overripens and rots and molds, the skin caves in, soft and mushy, the juices flow out, like the sticky mess of an uncontrolled bladder. This was the malignant outcome. The fate of Ion was his to share. Her abandonment of him had not been delayed; it was all the nearer, and I yearned to take him by the shoulders to tell him so. Yes, I did long to be that cruel. Jesse, instead, dallied in happiness, and I held my tongue, knowing my son's pain would only be all the worse when the osteal grin of the scythe-holder looked down on Natalia and stole her away.

4

I stared at a tree, the crimson leaves on its branches refusing to fall, the gusty wind having no effect. Grasses gold and brown mixed with yellowed leaves that were plummeting like a strange rain with no end. The petalled plants had long since shriveled up, curled in on themselves, turned brown, and had been whipped away with the wind, fragment by fragment, the beauty of each individual ripped to its smallest shreds. I turned my attention back to the page in front of me, a thing half full of words. Each sentence had been leading to this. I had done it, made a subject and set of facts lodged into the recesses of my cavernous memory essential to whatever came next, and there was no clean fashion for crawling out of the muddy corner which I'd written myself into, unless I had that which I had searched for now for months but had been unable to procure from my vast and outspread library. The book that contained some words, a paragraph, or a fresh take on Dardic elision was not to be found, and yet I had made myself unable to do without it.

Into the drain I emptied my full cup of coffee that I'd only but sipped. Jesse ran into the house, the front door slamming, his footfalls wild—seemingly everywhere—like hooves of horses pounding in stampede. Natalia appeared at my side, streaks of earth-colored paint on her hands, her hair knotted into a bun. "We should go to the pumpkin patch today," she said, washing the paint from her skin. Jesse came into the kitchen. "How was school?" Natalia asked. With overgenerous detail, Jesse recounted the events of his day.

"I want to play outside," he said.

"Actually," Natalia countered, "I was thinking we could go get pumpkins."

"Really?" he said. "I want a big pumpkin."

"Will you want to paint it or carve it?" she asked.

"I want to carve it, with a scary face," he said, opening his lips wide and raising his eyebrows in the way he pictured his pumpkin's face.

Natalia said, "Well, I was thinking maybe we could carve Billy into the face of the pumpkin."

"Feeding further this fish tale?" I said.

"I think it's a good idea. Besides, you bought him that figurine," she replied to me. "What do you think, Jesse? Do you want a scary pumpkin face or Billy the Lake Monster?"

"Lake monster!" he shouted.

"We'll have to get a really big pumpkin for your lake leviathan then," I said.

"Awesome."

"Do we have all the things we need for carving?" I asked Natalia.

"Yes, but we might need to pick up some tea lights."

We heard Jesse run up the stairs to deposit his backpack in his room and then heard him fly back down to us.

We stopped at a store along the way and picked up a package of four tea lights and then turned onto a road that wound its way west. The road was rural, flanked by trees and the occasional small farm where could be seen silos, dilapidated hen houses, and fences behind which lazed mud-splattered hogs or piebald goats. Natalia turned onto a gravel road where a sign—painted with a smiling pumpkin, the words *Pumpkin Patch* below it, and a pointing arrow—was planted in the sallow grass there along the road. We drove a ways down that thin course, a trail of dust blooming behind our vehicle, and eventually, to our right, the pumpkin patch appeared. In the distance, we saw figures walking around the dots of orange. As we neared, the view was obscured by pines. However, another sign loomed ahead, large and red, and on it was written the words *Turn Here*.

Natalia parked our car in the greener yard grass where other vehicles were lined in unmarked rows. Two pointing scarecrows directed us toward a large red barn. Inside were mostly families with children, and they walked around the tables and booths. Squash and gourds in various shapes and colors were for sale, as was a variety of baked goods, many containing pumpkin as an ingredient. There was a rack with paint kits for those who preferred not to knife away a face into their pumpkin. In one area, tea lights, holiday-themed coffee mugs, and hot apple cider were sold.

"Look," Natalia said, "we could've got tea lights here."

"See how expensive they are though," I said, pointing to the price.

Natalia had us buy some apple cider that was ladled into paper cups, which we sipped as we walked around. Jesse stopped in front of a row of small orange pumpkins displayed on stacks of square hay bales at the foot of which a big gray dog lazed.

"These are little pumpkins," I said to Jesse. "We'll get you a big one from the pumpkin patch."

"What's wrong with the dog?" Jesse asked.

"It's just tired."

"But what's she got on her?" he said, tilting his head.

There were tumors. The dog looked up at us with a tumorous blind eye and a good blue one and wagged its tail. I pet the dog on its head and said, "Just growths from old age." The dog wheezed from the attention and then lay back down and continued to pant with labored breathing.

Staffers in orange shirts hauled pumpkins in from the field on wagons and wheeled them to cars if they were very large or if more were bought than the family could carry. All transactions were processed at the great open doorway in the back of the barn. The atmosphere was one of integrity, there under the care of the smiling staffers, a place devoted to the nurturing of a festive milieu. People came and went without the oversight of security—only the omnipresence of courtesy.

We exited out of the back of that huge barn and walked through the pumpkin patch, examining the orange fruits. The field was bare but for the pumpkins that were spaced about, each cut by the stem from its vine. The dog trotted by, nose to the earth. Staffers helped with the pumpkins and answered questions. Children ran, screaming with excitement. A teenage couple passed us, holding hands. Jesse looked about for a pumpkin with warts and told us he wanted an old pumpkin with growths. I searched for the perfect pumpkin, round and smooth, and I thought of how we would bake its savory seeds. Natalia simply searched for the largest pumpkin she could carry in her arms.

A buzzing noise rushed by my ear. I saw a stinkbug fly in an uncertain, wobbly course, and I watched it as it passed into the distance, becoming a speck and vanishing into the background. It was the perfect symbol of this season—the last new lives of the year to be jotted down for the annals of birth as everything around wilted and died or sunk into a state of dormancy that could hardly be distinguished from death and, until the spring defrosted the iced bodies of the dormant at the animato direction of the day's warming airs, there could be no guarantee of rejuvenation, no guarantee that death had not taken hold during the snowy winter months. The spring was not just a time of life, it was a release of all that had been frozen, and it smelled of things dead, things that had been waiting out the snow so they could rot in the melt.

The point at which the stinkbug disappeared led my eye to view a pile of snarled vines, rotting pumpkins, and chopped tree limbs, which I knew, from previous year's visits to this same pumpkin patch, to be the refuse of the field. Large birds flew in a circle high above this spot. Lying at the foot of the mound I saw something unexpected. I walked to the end of the patch to examine what it was. It was the dog, its mouth hanging open, its tongue lying limp on the dirt, its one good eye open too wide. I picked up the dog like a sleeping child, and tears ran down my face. Natalia saw me and quickly came over.

"Honey?" she asked.

"The dog," I replied.

I walked through the field and past the pumpkins, unable to stop sobbing. A staffer in an orange shirt said, "Sir, put the dog down."

"The dog is dead," I blurted. "Out by the rotting pumpkins."

"Put the dog in the wagon. It's okay, sir."

"The dog?" I said.

"In the wagon, sir. We'll take care of her."

"Put it in the wagon, Robert," Natalia calmly ordered. I set the dog in the wagon and kept crying. "Go to the car," she instructed. I nodded and walked off, snuffling all the way to the car, and I waited there for my wife and son. They arrived with three pumpkins in a wagon pulled by an orange-shirted girl.

"Why were you crying?" Jesse asked after he crawled into the car.

Natalia answered, "Daddy was crying because the dog died."

"Why didn't you cry, Mom?"

"Your dad was fond of the dog. He'd known it since we first came to this pumpkin patch, oh, some years ago."

"I don't remember the dog," Jesse said.

"Your father does," she replied, and Natalia drove us with her eyes forward, watching the road the whole way home.

5

As a child, I shinnied the coarse trunks of trees, carrying a book in a backpack or clamped resolutely between my chin and chest. I'd sit in the boughs of shady retreat and dappled light up there where the wind blew through leaves, and the leaves were an instrument, accompanied by birdsong, and I'd read of dichotomous fairyland entities who struggled against one another. The hero's armor always shone, and he'd raise his double-edged sword above his windblown hair in righteous victory. The villain was always diabolical, sometimes of misshapen form and other times human, but beastly in nature; always the villain was intent on domination, always intent on fulfilling evil desires through evil deeds.

I'd look up only after finishing a chapter and notice the tree being joggled by an evening wind, and I'd turn my face to the west and observe the reddened sky and would mark the time by this beauteous sight. I'd lean back on my branch and imagine a hero come into existence. There should be heroes, I would think, heroes to rejuvenate the world gone brown and smoggy under the iron-mawed machines of crooked dictators. I had the idea that degradation of any kind—be it Third World poverty or the ripping away of nature's llanos and wildwoods—were setbacks. I had the notion that meliorism was the true nature of being. All it

would take to return the world to its right and hale
state was a hero who had risen from the trash-
littered grasses along the highwayland or who had
crawled from the labyrinthian world up through the
sewers into ours.

I would listen to cricket song, frog song, the
rattling of cicadas, and chew a last piece of bubble
gum as the planet spun me, and everything I knew,
toward evening.

I guessed that there were heroes out there yet
unnamed—martyrs stretched saltirewise, tortured,
unable to fight and, nevertheless, unwilling to
renounce their noble causes. I fantasized about
being a hero, about dying with joy in the glory of
agony. I wished it upon no one else, I swear.

I grew up and realized there were no heroes as I
had imagined, only varlets bumbling through life,
trying to serve the vacant suits of armor that were
bought at too high of a price and were made of
inferior things—the hinges rusting after the first run
through the dishwasher. I abandoned the books of
my childhood, and I read the classics where the
heroes do die, where sometimes there are no heroes.
My palate grew to lose all taste for saccharine magic;
I relished it only if it was real. The world got worse,
and then the body, like an extension of this abuse,
turned on itself. I dreaded the thought that Natalia
would have to suffer, that the cancer would ravage
her body in the end. A wasting disease it was called.
A slow death sentence is what it was. Carrying her

up a ladder and hanging her from a cross would be better than what she was to be given. If there were heroes, I would think they were the ones I love, but how is it possible for an antagonist to reside in the body of a beloved hero?

Life is villainy. Not the living of it, not the growing and the dying, the eating of life for sustenance, or how each step is a second closer to reaching final dysfunction. It is the experience of it. It is being conscious of it all. Life is life. And life must do what it must do. But why the knowledge of the act?

I looked up at a tree. I no longer climbed them. Traffic hummed by on the city street. There were children nearby, laughing and throwing a Frisbee. They had a dog with them. The dog would wait to see where the disc would land and then would take off and, by the time it got there, the Frisbee would be ready to throw again. It kept trying, the dog. It attempted, but it was not successful, and the children did not think to let the dog have the Frisbee just once. The dog did not pick up on the rhythm, did not adjust its pace and timing to the act of retrieval.

How many times must one try something before giving up on it?

The doctor had said it was too progressed. There was nothing to do. I kicked a rock. A car honked its horn in the empty street. I acquiesced in giving my consent of joinder to the audience simply awaiting her death. How did I view myself in light of this? How could I not question my character? So I shuffled along the sidewalk between the park and the street. Small, evenly spaced trees ran along the park side of the sidewalk. A few feet of empty grass bordered the street side. There was a soccer field in the park. I knew this because there were two blue-painted soccer goals facing each other with an expanse of brown grass in between. I stopped and stared at the soccer goals, though my mind was elsewhere.

Who was I? A man who had given up on companionship so easily so early. A man whose life was spent in study of dead words and whole dead languages, as if I was focused on abandonments larger than mine in an unconscious attempt to demonstrate that my own was nothing compared to this demitting of entire tongues. Yet I could not be so hard on myself, could I?

I turned around and retraced my steps. The trees there seemed identical and were spaced exactly apart. I imagined they were softwood trees. I could not envision my child-self in any of them. They were not the trees of my youth. They were saplings and, if not saplings, then cheap decoration for the park. I could not see them surviving another local drought or a real rush of wind.

No, it was not only I who had had enough—Natalia, too, understood the prognosis. She chose to cease any kind of treatment, to live her last days in advance rather than in retreat. She lived with the disease. She would die of the disease. All this was certain. And if there were a cure around the corner, to be found somewhere deep in the cabalistic archives, what of it? She would have to wrestle with mortality sometime. No more dirty tricks, chemicals or radiation. She would face the knowledge of her temporary existence clean and clear-headed, totally afraid.

I leaned against our car, willing the tears to recede. Then I opened the door, I got in, and I drove home.

6

I took another look at my office at the university. Framed diplomas hung on one wall, two paintings on the other. The oaken bookcase opposite the desk appeared starved, its shelves half empty, the places where the books had recently stood as free of dust as they were now free of the words entombed in the hardcover tomes. The desktop was barren, stripped of a studious scholar's productive clutter. The old office chair that I'd had since my early years in academia—a piece of a lost romance faded of original memory from too many others crossed atop it—would sit layered in the dust that fell gently and silently on all things in that room. I examined it and saw on the arms of the chair the worn varnish, rings of water stains, and the faded red of the seat's threadbare fabric, and I decided to pull it, slightly, from the desk, just as if someone had gotten up, intending to return momentarily. Natalia, like me, had been given leave of teaching duties that academic year, and I imagined nearly a year from then opening the office door and walking to that chair angled ready to take the whole of my body so I might rest my weary soul. Lastly, in the corner, was a small and unobtrusive spider, a tiny thing nearly translucent with long, wispy legs. I left it up there to

live and die as it would on the threads it spun like a
Norn of its own small fate.

Taking joy in the scent of the room, I inhaled. It
smelled like an old country porch—of paint chips
and a weathered swing, odorous of time spent lazing
away in the heat of a summer sun. Then I shut the
door, locked it, and dropped the key ring into my
coat pocket; it held keys that opened only certain
doors in the English department, doors I would not
be opening for a long time. I stood in the silent
hallway and listened, fancying I heard a page turn,
perhaps a book being read behind one of the doors;
if it were so, the reader did not cough or grunt or
make any other sound, and should I have stood and
listened for the turning of the next page, I would
likely have been there a long time.

The day was unusually warm, and inordinate
strings of web floated airborne, as though fate itself
was up in the air. New births of vicious beings with
jaws designed for carnivory were being hatched.
There was also an argosy of beetles and flies and
little creatures everywhere filling the air, preparing to
outwit the arachnids that parachuted in infant form
through those same limpid spaces. The air, I
realized, was thronged with life, and there would be
no numbering of the creatures that came alive that
day, nor would there be a tally of the deaths in the
wake of the spiders' viscid traps. As I walked, I saw
a lady on a bench, smoking a cigarette despite
campus regulation, and across her face were strands

of webs, three of them, caught on her right cheek and crossed to her left, one across the chin, one across the nose, and one across the brow, and they trailed into the breeze, waving like streamers. I lifted my hand to my nose and sneezed, and when I brought it down, I felt a sticky strand of web on my fingers.

"There is not a cloud in the sky," I said to myself, "and if there were, it would be but an aggregate of webbing balled into a white mass that was found flying in the lower winds of our atmosphere."

As I drove, I had many things to think about, none involving students or grading papers. All of my duties on campus had been transferred to others who were filling in for me. Some were teaching my classes, excepting those lectures on language and etymology that could not possibly be taught by any other of the staff in the department. I had only gone to campus that day to clear my office of some old files and books—a chore I had been neglecting— and to meet with a professor who had been teaching a class of mine since August. He was excited to be teaching the class, but had wanted to meet to clarify some points of understanding on a thick text assigned toward the latter half of the semester.

As we were parting, he had said to me, "I'm sending my prayers."

I turned and asked, "To which gods?"

He smiled and chuckled and shook his head.

I told him, "Just don't send us flowers."

I looked at the road before me. Leaves lined the curbs, a drifting of autumnal refuse. I glanced at the houses as I drove past them and observed pumpkins on porches and lining doorsteps. Hanging about the houses on windows and door fronts were cartoonish ghouls that bore little resemblance to the actual forms that horror takes in life, and there slipped over me then a sense of relief. I had been given time to spend with my wife and she time to be with her family. It seemed strange to feel a sort of pleasant warmth at the thought that there was not to be a hospital-bound end for Natalia. There would be no gurney; instead, she would lay on her own familiar bed, and the food would be cooked in the pots and pans of our kitchen, and her death would be marked with tragedy and meaning, with no white hospital walls or tired nurse to claim her death as quotidian, even if quotidian death may be. It was not hardihood or denial of the deterioration we would see in her condition that made us believe she was better off with the comforts of home, rather than with machines and medicines meant for the prolongation of life. It was planning for the end. A plan laid out, at least, on our own terms.

But woe was not to be forgone. Reality was no masker knocking on the door and dividing choice into two disparate options of trick or treat. With a stolid, clean-shaven visage sporting a thin pair of exsanguinous lips, Reality knocked, delivered words as a bearer of news and spoke the facts with objectivity, like the recitation of a scientific study or a law document. Without irony, Reality glanced at his wristwatch, looked up and smiled, his report done, and he inquired, "Anything else?" What could we say to such a thing, to the facts of the situation? Could we implore God or Satan or science to offer us another option? Yes, we could, but there would be no dignity in that, and in the end, we would be able to say: "At least we had dignity. At least this one thing was salvageable."

So I drove home happy and sad, both at the same time—happy to have her, sad to lose her. The future looked dim, despite the bright fact of our present together. That it hurt, sometimes, to feel happy is what I found hardest to explain to her when we lay in our bed long after our lights were out, whispering our thoughts to one another late into the night.

I parked the car outside the garage, thinking I would take some time to wash the vehicle by hand on what might have been the last available warm day. I took a moment to look around, and I saw that the trees were almost bare with some red or gold leaves clinging to a branch here and there, but they fluttered in the smallest zephyrs and would not hold much longer, and, in the woods around the lake, could be spotted the dense green of conifers once hidden by the obscuration of a thousand living green leaves. Directly above the house was a somber cloud that floated with a dark underbelly. It held no company and seemed ready to prove itself an adversary to the bright day with the mustering of fulgurous stirrings within. I cared not to look up at the thing for long; instead, I observed the house and saw that Jesse and Natalia had raked the leaves into two piles, one at each end of the yard, and on the front doorstep were our three pumpkins. Natalia's was the silhouette of a Halloween cat. Jesse's was his lake monster that his mother outlined onto the pumpkin before she helped him cut into the shell. Mine was a classic jack-o'-lantern with jagged teeth and two triangular eyes. I smiled, thinking on how after I had cleared out the inside and refined the sharp edges of each tooth, I had stepped back and declared it was a ferocious pumpkin.

I exhaled happily and was satisfied. I went inside to find Jesse so he could help me wash the car. "Jesse," I called.

"We're in the kitchen, Robert," my wife hollered back. I walked into the kitchen and saw, at the table, my son, my wife, and a man in a blue shirt. "This is Charles Yearwood," she said and then slowly added, "the architect who lived here and renovated the house before us."

A cold sweat washed over my body.

"Hello," he said.

"Charles, this is my husband, Robert."

"Nice to meet you, Mr. Yearwood."

"Please have a seat," he said, as if I needed an invitation. He was bald with thick cheeks, though he had strong craftsman's arms. He wore dress pants and black tennis shoes. Then he turned to my son and said, "As I was trying to say, that's the thing, Jesse, Heaven is an empty stillness. It's not black or white but the color of emptiness. Immutable in its qualities. Incorruptible in its eternity. It is this that I fled from when making my alterations to the house. I needed to dig deeper into the walls for that constancy of movement and to hide from what will kill me. Stillness *is* death. You see the practicality of my process, of what I have done?"

My son nodded, although I knew he did not understand what Charles was saying. And I became angry. Had my son asked him about Heaven? And even if he had, who was this man to spout theology? My wife looked at me with wide eyes. Her hands gripped the edge of the table. She pointed with her chin, and I rose from my chair. Her cue failed; the architect followed me into the living room. "You've got a good family, yes, sir, you do," he said.

"Thank you, Mr. Yearwood," I replied.

"Jesse, go upstairs," Natalia said, blocking him from following.

"Mom?"

"To your room," she said.

"How long have you lived here?" he asked. We walked in a circle around the room with him lingering about two paces behind me.

Natalia watched from the entrance to the living room. She answered him, "About a year after you...moved out. The place stood empty for a while. They had trouble selling it."

"You have so many books," he said.

"You should see the library," Natalia replied.

"Yes, I should. Library you say?" He looked at her curiously. It was obvious he did not know of any such room.

"Come," Natalia said. She walked him to the large room where the lion's share of our books lined the walls.

"Oh," he said, "this was my studio. I had drawings and drafting tables here. In that area I had scale models I was working on. And over here," he said, sweeping his arms to show us, "I kept a filing cabinet. It was full of sketches and blueprints. It was right here. Do you happen to know where it has gotten off to? I would really, really like to work on them again if I could."

"I'm sorry," I said, "there was nothing in the house when we moved in. Maybe you've a relative who took care of your belongings?"

"Relative?" he asked, and then he shook his head, squinting his eyes at me. "I don't think so." He waved his hand, dismissing my apparently outlandish suggestion, even though I knew this was, in fact, what had happened.

Natalia again caught my eye and thrust her chin at me. The architect bent down to look at something on a shelf. "What a curious portent," he said. "Quite the photograph, huh?" He lifted the picture of Natalia that I had set there leaning against the framed photograph of the three of us. He studied the snapshot and looked at the back of it and then flipped it to the front again and said, "I wonder who took this?"

"I need to go to the bathroom," I said.

As I walked past, Natalia squeezed my hand and whispered to me, "He was in the house. In the walls, singing to himself."

"I'll call the authorities," I whispered back. In the bathroom I phoned them and told them that there was an intruder, apparently benign, but that we believed him to be the former resident who probably had escaped from the asylum in the south of the state.

I went back downstairs and told Charles Yearwood and my wife, "We'll have other visitors knocking on the door soon." Charles was still plodding around the library, the photograph in his hand.

"You must have renovated a lot of houses in your time," Natalia said.

"Yes," he replied. "Yes, I did. Though none compared to this house. This was my great work. My grand project. However, it was not finished."

"The half-built wall," I guessed.

"In the basement, yes. That was where I left off, and there was to be more."

"More? What was it you didn't finish?"

The architect lifted his head and with a sad smile said, "The final hiding place. Had I completed it, I never would have had to leave. Not God himself could've caught me."

I could not say why, but I challenged this statement—this crazy statement from a crazy person. "Tell me," I asked, "how could anyone hide from God?"

"The infinite enfilade," he said. "Had I finished, I could have opened every door, wall, and sliding panel, and they would have curved just so," he said, using his hands to illustrate this curve envisioned in his mind, "so that one would lead to another, and I could forever run through, unendingly winding about the house. I was so close to this dream, so close to forfending myself from the terror of that final peace."

I could see it, all the hidden entrances and exits leading to one another as an interconnected weave of wood and walls forming this strange structure. I could envision him with all the doors flung open, every passage unhinged, all the black mouths behind the false walls open and ready to receive the runner. Yes, I could see how he was so close, but it wasn't complete. His last hidden doorway was not cut, and his final walls were yet to be built, were only half-finished. I was about to ask which was the first door and what final renovations were there for this scheme of unending motion when the police knocked on the front door and took Charles Yearwood away.

We let Jesse play in the house that day with a friend but would not them play outside because we were understandably on edge after the surprise visitor's visit, and we talked about the architect over cups of steaming tea.

Natalia shook her head and said, "What a strange man."

"Well," I said, "he is in an asylum for a reason. Yet he seemed to carry a latent intelligence. You could say it even peeked through."

"His ideas were beyond eccentric in my opinion. All of his mannerisms and the way he talked were just weird. He was singing in the walls. Humming some tune. I thought it was Jesse at first, and when I opened up the wall, there he was, this man."

"But his words," I said, "were not unlearned."

She squinted at me and cocked her head. "He did have quite the vocabulary."

"Yes he did. I liked how he used *forfend* cleverly. Instead of Heaven forfending him, he was forfending himself from Heaven. A reversal of the typical usage. But intentional wit?"

Natalia shrugged. "And look at this house," she said, "so much inner space. We must utilize a third of the house's actual room. To do what he has done to this place, he must be a genius."

"A genius with the plague of insanity."

"A fear."

"Of death," and we looked at each other and averted our eyes like strangers.

In the evening we three went out in our jackets, intending to eat a late supper in town. Above us were streaks of crumbling purple clouds, and the sun was a gold dome sinking into the earth. I pointed at the lawn and said, "Look," for in the grass there was a lambent shimmering of spiderwebs that danced like a mirage on the road. Not an inch of our yard was spared this opalescence, and we took it to be propitious because it was beautiful and because we were only human and could be enchanted by the spectacle, by the illusory masquerade of nature's wondrous ways.

A velleity for happiness, a velleity for sleep. I lay awake and unhappy while a night wind blew through the skeletal trees and hit the house with a long, empty howl. There were no chirring insects, no twittering of nighttime fowl. The heavy blankets weighed like cold earth over me, and I shivered in my underclothes. I touched Natalia's bare back gently with the tips of my fingers, and I felt the movement of her body with my hand as she breathed with long, gentle breaths. I removed my touch and turned away. Sliding from the bed and rising to my feet, I stood in the moonlight like a creature begotten ex nihilo, pushed forth from the fabricless womb of night. I tiptoed to the door and turned the handle slowly and, hearing the soft snap of the latch, I opened the door partway and went out into the hall, and then I shut the door with careful, slow movements, not wishing to wake up Natalia. I walked down the dim hall, colder now, and I wished I had grabbed a robe to wear. I found the thermostat and, in the paltry light, turned up the heat. I waited a few moments and then heard the distant buzz of the furnace coming to life and seconds later heard the gush of warm air exhaling from the vents. A creak sounded, and I turned and saw a sliver of dark that was darker than the black around it. I stood nearly nude with no faith and no apotropaic cross or charm should what was before me be some form of vagile evil, real only during that dreaming hour. I looked and knew I would have to investigate, for the dark sliver was located along a wall the way I had come, and I could not pass and let it be. I moved with slow footfalls and stopped every couple steps to observe if any change had occurred in that line of dark against the wall. I understood that it must be a shadow, but a shadow of what, I asked myself, and why did it, although but a line of black, seem so uncanny, and why was its appearance proceeded by a single creaking note, like the fanfare of a specter rising from its tomb? Then there it was before me, and I stood face to face with the lightless line interpolated like an unfamiliar stick of furniture in my home. I reached out my hand, offering my digits to the dark and to discovery. In they went, and my thumb hooked the edge of the dark, and I opened the night that the wall contained, and it opened with a groan that spoke of sore disuse and sounded of abandonment.

I stepped into the void. It could only have been another passageway undiscovered by us three who resided in the house. I assumed that Charles Yearwood, while wandering through his old maze of secret doors, had used this one and thus loosened the panel and disrupted its airtight grip, and when I turned on the furnace, some change in air pressure had forced open the wall. A reek of stale air was followed by the smell of woody dust, like the scent of a derelict farmhouse. Webs thick, like cotton, caught at my arms and clung to my toes. I moved forward, blind, with my arms swinging invisible in the lightless air. The space was wide, and if I stood in the middle with my arms outstretched to the sides, they found no wall until I leaned a little to the right or left. The floor was smooth, perhaps tile. I strained my ears to hear a howling. It was faint and I guessed it to be the murmur of the wind outside. Nothing crawled on me, even as more webs clung to my body, and I imagined this space empty of life— little carcasses rotted to dust after cannibalizing one another or starving each on its own dust-laden web, an ecosystem enclosed and unable to feed itself. Of course, I could have been wrong, though it did not matter because spiders were not the thing I feared.

I stopped, the toes of my left foot finding only half a floor. I stepped back, dizzy. I went to my knees and then to my belly. The floor was freezing against my bare skin, and still I crawled forward, feeling with my hands. Then there it was—a ledge. My fingers gripped it, and I let them crawl down its sides, expecting I would find the projection of a step. I found none. To reach farther down, I pulled myself closer to the edge, facing the black below, and I could sense cold air rising from down there and, from the unreachable space of the deep, I heard the sound of an arctic breath spilled in an unending note as if it were the sacred om of reality contemplating reality, and my eyes stung with tears at the notion that this diligent mentation could be the cyclical act that sustained all of existence.

I swept my arms along the ledge, and I felt something protruding, determining it to be the rung of a ladder, and it seemed to be made of wrought iron. My arms could reach only two rungs down. I pulled at the ladder and found it to be unmovable, somehow fastened to the wall of the ledge. I lowered a bare foot onto the first rung, and it felt dirty with oxidation. Facing as I was, I looked at the entrance but could not see it; all I perceived was a depthless black, and my eyes built phantasms of shifting colors as they attempted to construct an image on the surfaceless dark. I shut my eyes and lowered my other foot, but before it reached the second rung, I abandoned the ladder to the possible abyss and ran out into the hall, shutting the wall and its secrets behind me. "I will find you in the morning," I whispered to myself.

I cleaned the brown cobwebs off of me and turned, scanning myself in the mirror, and I balled up each clump of webbing in my hands and washed them down the bathroom drain. After this, I carefully crawled back into bed where my wife slept soundly, dreaming of mundane activities, like searching for her phone to check the time—in her dream she is in our house, yet it is not exactly our house but also a natatorium. I am swimming. She calls to me, but I keep diving down to the bottom of the pool, and I spring up out of the blue to an impossible height, my body vertical, each time higher than the last. I am wearing bright red trunks and a daydreamlike smile so big that all my teeth show. She yells, "Honey, do you know where my phone is?" I poke my head up like a spy-hopping dolphin, my face now washed of all emotion, and I dive back down, deep into the blue until I am a shadow swimming the length of the pool. Frustrated, she turns around to search for the phone elsewhere.

The morning greeted me with a soft light and an empty bed. I lay there in a nirvanic state, letting the peaceful feeling of my mind and body awakening flow around me in slow drips like dilatory time. Slowly those drips began to fall faster until the hands of the clock once again spun at a normal pace, and I was able to join my mind to the tangible world. I donned a robe and went downstairs, sniffing; the smell of batter and butter was in the air, and my stomach growled in response.

"Hey, honey, glad you're up. Could you finish squeezing the oranges while I do these last pancakes?" Natalia smiled at me.

I called Jesse into the kitchen for breakfast, and we ate pancakes with maple syrup and drank the fresh orange juice. "I just remembered," I said, "last night I found another secret passage."

"No. Really? You're kidding."

"Where?" Jesse asked.

"In the hallway to our bedroom. It opened when I turned on the furnace."

"I thought we found them all," Natalia said.

"Yeah, I should look into it. I didn't go very far."

"You went into it?"

"Uh-huh."

"Anything interesting?"

"Nothing that I could see. It was dark."

"You think he was in there?"

"He must have been. Why else would it have opened after all these years?"

"It makes you wonder what else we possibly haven't discovered. Of course, if we haven't discovered it, we won't miss it. Will we? Still, I like to think we know our own home. It's unsettling that we don't. Or that we don't know it totally. Fully. This is Mr. Yearwood's grandest piece of art, and we don't utilize it as such. We turn it into a domestic sphere—which it is meant to be on the one hand, but it's also so much more. At least, now, I get his intentions."

"Do you? Is his design artistic or theological?"

"Does it matter, Robert? Even today lots of art is inspired by religion or is religious. Secularization of art is actually a rather new phenomenon. Early art wasn't detached from mysticism or magic. I'm like talking about cave paintings and whatnot. Idol carving also. These were acts of magic. And, really, who's to say making art isn't still magical today?"

"Are you saying that magic and religion are the same?"

"Of course they're one and the same," Natalia said. "They're both based on the notion of the supernatural. Religion and magic each require belief in something that cannot be empirically proven. Mysticism, or whatever historians call it, is the older understanding of how the world operates. In the grand history of our species, it is actually mysticism, artistic mysticism, that reigns. So if I were to choose a religion, I'd choose art because the act of making art is still endowed with belief, with magic. I know that our society may say the opposite, but come on, just because we accept the idea of artistic inspiration as a right brain phenomena doesn't mean it isn't a form of mysticism. Think about it. Inspiration? The muse? Aren't we really talking about religious conceptions?"

"Has my wife become a believer?"

"God no. Or vice versa, I should clarify. The very nature of being human means attempting to come to terms with the world in an explanatory way. Atheists or not, we artists are still the original high priestesses, shamans, or whatever. In touch with the divinity encoded in everyone's genes."

"Amen," I laughed, having thoroughly enjoyed my wife's lecture. I cleared the table and, still in my robe, I walked to the hall and observed the wall. It, again, was seamless and had the appearance of being impregnable, outside the use of a saw or sledgehammer. With roseate confidence, I ran my finger along it, hoping to catch the crack where the panel must have moved. I found no screw to turn, no thumbhole to press, no ornamentation or molding fixed to its space where lifting or pulling it could cause the shifting of levers to unlatch the hidden door. I wondered that I had never before discovered some mechanism to reveal this chamber. If it was simply an object built into the décor of the house, surely some accident would have already made apparent the wall's false fixity. The panel could not be controlled by a knob, for every knob we had seen had been turned. So its *switch* was small, discreet. I looked and looked, and I could find no mechanism. I turned up the heat, and the furnace kicked on and still the wall remained shut without so much as a shudder.

My wife walked by, heading toward the bedroom and asked, "Any luck?"

I replied, "No. My question is, if he was in there, did he get in through the conveyance of a connecting passage or by entering the hall itself?"

"I don't know," she said. "Guess you shouldn't have shut it."

"Guess you're right."

Jesse came by, and he was curious and eager to help, so we both began to clear books from the shelves in the hallway and to move furniture away from the walls, revealing every inch of panel and baseboard. Though we ran our fingers along the walls like blinded prisoners of war in the *cachot* below the feet of Assyrian throne-masters, we found no depression, no latch, or any moving part to open the door.

Natalia came out of the bedroom, dressed and wearing makeup. "I'm going out to buy some new paint brushes," she said. She stepped around the books and shelves that we moved to the middle of the floor. "Maybe it was a dream," she said. Natalia stopped and leaned against the wall and told us of the dream she had that morning of where there was a swimming pool in the house, and she said she had other dreams too, lots of them, but they had already drifted off like insubstantial air bubbles floating down a sylvan-shaded stream, too ephemeral to remain vivid to the one who dreamed them. She stepped over a final pile of books and left to buy the brushes.

I placed my ear against the cool wall and listened. I could not distinguish the sound of blood pulsing in the veins of my ear from that of the slow exhalation of the deep well that had been sealed shut. Like a seashell, I heard the false ocean roaring in me. I looked to Jesse and said, "I suppose it doesn't matter." He looked disappointed, and I was sorry for my son who longed for an answer after the morning's hard work, but the time had expired for the charnel to cough up its bones.

With everything moved away from the walls, we took the opportunity to clean away the cobwebs and wipe away the dust, turning the search for a secret embedded in the structure of our home into the prosaic act of sweeping up the dirt. I thought of dirt as I cleaned—I thought of farmers' plows slicing into it to seed the soil, and I thought of my childhood, of mud pies and my arms up to my elbows in sand, and I thought of the dead we put there in the ground and covered with the earth.

7

We drove to the graveyard, my wife and I. Jesse was at school. We packed food for a simple picnic: sliced grilled chicken, seedless red grapes, rotini pasta salad, bottled water, and coffee in a thermos. The day was cold, and we wore coats and stocking caps. Blue-colored clouds, like sheets of colossal ice, furrowed the sky. A paved road ran through the cemetery. My wife's plot was in a newer section of that expansive graveyard, atop a hill tucked up next to a woods. Facing her headstone properly—with one's back to the trees—gave an impressive view of the graveyard below and the horizon beyond.

I parked the car, and we both got out. There were no dead on that hill yet. It had room for maybe a dozen plots. Headstones were placed here and there and, like my wife's, they lacked an epitaph, for it was only contracts and preparedness that claimed the land for those graves. Some blank stones were sunk low into the ground and others slanted so that a visitor could easily, one day, be able to read the words that would be engraved upon them. Very near the trees was a solitary obelisk made of brownish sandstone that matched the woods behind it, and I wondered if the plants would creep forward and encroach upon this little monument over time or if the groundskeepers would cut back the woods to expand the laying places for the dead. Natalia's tombstone was classic in shape. It was of a bronzy granite and, in the sun, glinted with flecks of mica. She walked up to her stone and then walked away from it, backward. She stepped to the left and then to the right and then took a sideways step. "Here," she said, "Bring my chair, please." I did, and she placed it in the spot where she stood. Then we walked to the car, and we unloaded her canvases and the supplies she needed for painting. She adjusted her chair and easel and began by looking out at the view in front of her.

I pulled out a second chair, unfolded it, and set it away from Natalia, closer to the trees where I could be both in the sunlight and protected from the nipping breeze. I poured coffee from the thermos into two insulated travel mugs. I brought one to Natalia, and she thanked me. I took mine to my chair, and I sat and read. I heard the breeze passing through the nearly naked limbs of the trees, which shivered just slightly like many cold, uncoated arms. After some time, a lone bird began to twitter in the woods and this roused me to refresh our coffees. "How is it coming?" I asked upon returning her mug.

"Good. I don't know." She sighed. She had started a second canvas. The first one lay face up in the grass.

"Want me to take that to the car?" I said, pointing.

"Leave it, please. I need it to know what I did wrong."

I became absorbed in my book. While I read, the words seemed to pulse, darker and then brighter, in the subtle changes of light as the clouds crossed the sky in unbroken silence. The bird quit its song in midnote, and I looked up from my book at the half-finished painting of her burial land. Natalia dipped her brush into the paint, and she touched the canvas with it, erasing color from the skyline, for her brush had been wet with acrylic white. I focused again on the narrative I was reading. A gust of wind whistled through the branches and then a bird cawed in the trees, and, some seconds later, I heard it land on the ground in the woods, which was covered in leaves. The bird gave another raspy caw, and I heard its overt hops across the leaf fall. A third time I heard its call, and a second bird interjected with its own piercing voice. Then there were more, and they chattered and soon there was an uproar in the woods as more birds of the same kind joined in jubilation.

I rose and put the book on the seat of my chair. Natalia continued to paint. I walked to the edge of the woods and looked into the trees. The birds were hopping around and opening their beaks to caw, as though they were performing a primal religious rite. As they moved, they hopped not just over the ground, but over something else too. The birds were large, and if they were crows, they were crows of amazing size. They were black and sported knifelike beaks. For a few moments, the birds scattered enough for me to see that the thing they jumped on was a body. What type of body, I did not know, but it had a gray coat, which looked wet and dirty. I caught sight of one sable eye and perhaps a fang jutting from a slightly parted lip, and I thought the tooth doglike in appearance, though the body was both wild and unwolfish at once. I did not venture to guess at the origins of such a creature and what it may have hunted. The birds cawed between their hops and between their pecking at the corpse, and with their beaks they began to rip the flesh of the animal, for these birds were scavengers and this was their meal. They ate and they cawed and they cawed and they cawed, and their cawing was more than the call of feasters, it was also an epithalamium honoring the marriage of the soul to its eternal deathmate.

I walked over to my wife and said, "Painting number four."

"It's all wrong," she said.

I looked at the paintings and shook my head. Art of the visual kind was not my subject, but I could see something was certainly missing from the paintings. The headstone was there, the trees, the grass, and sky. "You're trying to paint your death," I said.

"And here I am. I've got the gravestone. A great graveyard view. I just don't know what's off with these paintings."

"They're missing you."

She nodded her head. "Let's go," she said. We packed up our things, and decided it was getting too cold to eat outside, so we picnicked in the car, and though the car doors and windows were closed, we heard the birds eating their meal while we chewed ours without words.

Natalia asked me, "What's the matter? You never seem to work on your manuscript anymore."

I was having trouble with my own art. The most I could accomplish was the x-ing out of paragraphs. It all seemed folly.

"It's frustrating," I replied. I was trying that morning to accomplish something, but my pen failed to elicit words. Instead, I stared at the six vases that had accumulated on my desk, and I wondered why we let dead flowers linger everywhere about the house. It was too much work to dry all of them, and Natalia had quit that task some time before. I felt I was overwhelmed with many things—the book I was writing, or trying to write, the ticking away of time—and yet time was given to me in abundance. It was only the structuring of time properly that caused me anxiety. I'd ask myself: How much time do I spend with Natalia? How much time do I spend having coffee with a colleague or chatting with a brilliant student? How much time do I spend at any particular task? Wasn't the task of tossing the farewell flowers supposed to be an act of closure anyway, not something meant to be done while she walked the halls of the house and squeezed my hands and kissed my brow and lips?

Unable to write, I went out gift shopping for the associate dean whose birthday was approaching. While out, I ran into a professor from the department. I had selected an hourglass made by a local glassblower and was waiting in line to purchase the curio. The man ahead of me turned and said, "Robert."

"Porter."

"How are you?"

"Good, yeah."

"I've been meaning to get around," he said. "Just never stopped by, you know. Isn't this a great little store?"

"I love it."

"It's nice that there's a place for the locals to sell their crafts."

"It is," I said. "There's certainly a lot of talent."

"I was just getting something for the old lady. It's our anniversary. She says she doesn't want a thing; I know better. Why are you here? Where's the wife?"

"She's at home. I'm buying this for Charlene's birthday." I held up the hourglass.

"Say, that's nice."

"Think she'll like it?"

"For sure. She can use it to pace our department meetings." He turned back to the clerk. "Thank you," he said and then, "Hey, Robert, you up for a coffee? I've got time."

"Why not," I nodded and instructed the clerk to go ahead and gift-wrap the present.

"You sure? I don't want to hold you up."

"I'm good. I've nothing else particular planned. Found what I came out to get," I said.

"Wonderful. Been to the Purple Diner before?"

"Yeah."

"Yeah, but have you had their coffee?"

"No."

"Wicked good cup. Let's walk. Just up the street anyhow," he said. "And hey," Porter said, turning to the clerk, "you're a peach. Thanks again." The clerk blushed and bid us farewell.

Porter taught ancient classics at the university and had written probably more books on the *Oresteia* than any living writer. He was tall with a sagging gut and had a prominent nose. Porter was bald but for a few long and wiry gray hairs. He always dressed in blazers, even on days he didn't teach, and he was known on campus for his extreme intelligence and having high expectations of his students.

We took a booth at the diner and he ordered us coffees. "How is the wife, Robert?" he asked, relaxed in the corner of his seat, one arm resting on the windowsill.

"She's doing fairly well," I said.

"Hum. It's a real shame, Robert. I heard it's terminal."

"We battled her cancer twice," I said, "and we can't do it a third time."

"Really?"

I shook my head. "It's everywhere. It's too progressed."

"Jesus Christ," Porter said. Our coffee arrived. "Thank you, Mary," he smiled at the waitress. She walked off, and I blew on my coffee to cool it some. "You know I lost my first wife. My daughter, Cassie, is actually hers—not Patricia's. Lost her in a plane crash of all things."

"I didn't know."

"It hurt right here," Porter said, holding a fist over his heart. "Flying back from a job interview. Hit a flock of birds. I guess there were thousands. Something about the weather that year got them all going. I don't know. I was devastated. It was bad. Real bad."

"Yeah?"

Porter took a drink from his cup. "That's my story."

I sipped from my cup. "Hey, this is good coffee," I said.

"The Purple Diner is where it's at. You know you're not like me. You're older than I was when I lost my wife. Wiser. Sagacious. That's what you are

Robert, you're sagacious. Heartbreak though, that's a tough thing. It can get a man down."

"I've experienced loss before," I said.

"I hit the bottle hard. I'm being honest here. I did. You know," he laughed, "I could see you hitting the wine pretty hard."

"There's always that danger." I smiled.

"I'm being serious here, Robert. Okay, do a little drinking if you must, but, if possible, just don't. This is experience talking here. My little Cassie lost both her parents for a while. You've got a son. What's his name?"

"Jesse."

"Jesse. You've got Jesse to think about. You'll both be hurting, but at least you've got each other. No drink can replace that bond there."

"I appreciate the advice, Porter."

"Well, you probably didn't need it."

"I don't know. I like my wine. My wife does too. I'll be lucky if there's any left in the house by year's end the way we're going, what with no papers to grade."

"I'm partial to dry wines myself," he said. "Partial to beer really."

"Definitely stop over sometime before the wine collection is completely depleted," I invited.

"That'd be good. I could bring over a nice merlot or, better yet, a nice India pale ale for you and Natalia to try."

I wondered if he'd keep good on his offer; he rarely made social calls, despite the fact he was frequently invited. Though he was a loquacious character in public, I could envision him going home, grading papers, and then delving yet again into one of his Greek tragedies and, becoming inspired by some word or phrase or incongruity, taking up his pen and getting lost in composition—a habit, I imagined, that brought to a close that period of heavy drinking induced by his personal tragedy.

I sighed. "It must have been tough. Being without your wife. Going out after she had gone. I suppose, though—well, I don't suppose—but…do you believe you'll see her again?"

"You mean like in the afterlife? You know, Robert, all those images, we created them. We create symbols. Harps and clouds and haloes, a visage of an eternity that isn't. Harps—an idea that an earthly instrument would be used to praise God. Clouds—because those of limited imagination thought Heaven really was up in the sky. Our Christian notion of the holy nimbus comes from Homer mostly."

"And what of an angel's wings?"

"Less symbolic than you might think. They stem from Biblical descriptions of cherubim and seraphim. Winged beings. Assumed to be angels of a higher order."

"And the dead, when did they don wings?"

"Men see patterns. It's all patterns. Cherub to angel to dead soul. We connect what is unrelated."

"So the pattern has nothing to do with reality?"

"The pattern *is* reality. It is man's. Man is the pattern and the pattern is man. Without man to make a pattern there'd be no such patterns."

"Do you deny the reality of fractals?" I asked.

"Those patterns of nature?"

"Yes."

"Shapes. All things take shape. And if there is repetition, it is godless."

"So you're saying nature has jurisdiction over its own animation."

"Yes, it does. Over its own configurations. If a pattern is helpful, then a pattern it will be. But it cannot be recognized as such without man," he said.

"Man puts wings on angels and on the dead of men. *Deo pleni sunt omnes hominess*," I declared.

He paid for the coffee, and I thanked him and he thanked our waitress. Then I walked back to my car, alone.

In the air was the smell of smoke drifting across the lake from the first fall fires. Some of those fires would be stoked the winter long with the laying of new logs on andirons, and the fires would be fed from the cords of wood stored in places protected from the moistures of rain and snow so that they would burn dry and hot and combat the bite of winter's icy jaws. I stood at the edge of the lake and watched the smoke curl, toddling leisurely upward, deliberate and sure of its place, smudging the sky. I thought of how the world began in fire and how in fire the world would end, leaving a screen of smoke and ash to inherit it all in perfect absolution. Jesse was away at a sleepover and Natalia was shut away in her studio. I had no words to add to any tome so I let the lapping of the water at the lake's edge lull me while the sky grew darker and the air colder as the sun steadily plunged into the blue-hilled horizon.

I went back to the house and prepared my simple homemade mocha—coffee, hot milk, cocoa powder, and a little chocolate sauce to sweeten it. I made two mugs and was about to take the one to Natalia when I heard her call for me. I walked carefully to where she was, carrying both cups in my hands. She was standing in the doorway to her studio. "Robert," she said, "I have finished a painting."

"That so?" I said.

"It is." She came to me and took a mug from my hand. "I'll even let you see it…for a kiss."

"That's awfully high admission," I said. "Perhaps just a peck on the cheek."

"No, no, no. One whole kiss, smack on the lips. It's a half-off discount, just for today. Grand-opening discount. Normally it's two kisses."

"This gallery needs a grant to fund itself. I'm a college professor. I can't afford your admission price," I said and turned around.

"You get back here and give me a kiss, Robert." She grabbed my arm, and I turned and gave her a long, impassioned kiss.

I went into the room, and Natalia followed behind me. The painting was on its easel and the last drops of paint were drying. It was of two women, one large and the other small. The large woman stood and looked down as if into herself, a curl of a smile gracing her lips, her cheeks full and blushed. The small woman knelt facing the spectator. Her eyes were two tormented pleas. Her hair was wild, thin. She was frail, an emaciated figure, nude to the world. This small woman was encompassed by the large woman. They were one woman and two at once, aspects of an inner world and an outer appearance.

Natalia leaned toward me. "It's called *Woman with Cancer*," she whispered. It was a masterpiece, and it was her final painting.

8

The clouds hung high, and the sun pulsed through the milky wash above at long intervals, like a sign of the drawn-out slowdown of the sun's heliometabolism. It was jacket weather. Birds chirped in the woods. A woodpecker flew from tree to tree to mark its territory with its pounding.

"Goal!" I shouted at Jesse. He ran for the ball that was rolling away from him. The sun began shining, and the lake went from blue to yellow and then back again. Jesse kicked the ball to me. We did this sometimes, played soccer out in the yard, a two-man scrimmage. To mark the goals, we had little flags, the ones utility workers used to spot the lines they painted in grass. Natalia had grabbed four of them one day, declaring the number of flags littering our yard to be excessive and, so, had purloined them for Jesse. We had a red, an orange, and two yellows.

My nose was cold and a bit runny, but the rest of me was warm from our play, and I discarded my jacket, and we laughed and yelled as we ran, kicking the ball around the yard. Overhead we heard the engine of an airplane lost to sight. A dog barked somewhere on the banks of the New Bedford Lake. The sound carried across the water and into our game. It was a natural noise, this barking. It did not disrupt or concern us. It was what dogs did, just like birds soared on the winds and ants dug elaborate tunnels in the earth. Then the dog stopped its lone bays of alarm, and I stopped also.

"It's break time for this old man," I said.

"I want to stay outside and practice."

"Okay. You practice. Work on your defense," I joked.

"All right," he said.

I laughed and picked up my jacket from the grass and went inside. The house was warm. There was the smell of banana bread baking in the oven. I saw the electric timer counting down the minutes. I flung my jacket on the back of a kitchen chair and went upstairs to change my shirt. On the bedside table was an old book I had been reading. I picked it up and smelled the foxed pages—a small pleasure. The paper was soft and the typeface a style outdated before I was born. A sound reached my ear, and I turned my head to better catch it. It kept beeping. I realized it was the sound of the timer calling out for the baker.

I picked out a clean shirt and tossed the other into the hamper and went downstairs to the kitchen. The timer sang out its insistent note. After finding an oven mitt, I pulled open the oven door, stepped back, and let the heat roll out, wrinkling the air for a second, and then I removed the pan with the bread and set it on the stovetop. I grabbed a toothpick, pierced the center of the bread, and then pulled it out to make sure it was done. It was. I set the toothpick on the counter and turned off the oven. Then I shut off the timer and I called out, "Natalia."

I went to the living room. The sun brightened. There were motes floating everywhere, thousands of them, each insignificant, without soul or purpose, like leftovers of reality's formation. I walked to the window. The sun dimmed. Jesse was outside. He tried to bounce the ball on his knee. I watched him kick the ball toward the water. He picked up the ball, and he watched the lake. I moved away from the window, and I walked out of the room.

I peeked into her studio. There was a new canvas, a blank one, on the easel. Her last painting was moved to the side, leaning against a wall. A clock struck the waning hour, the sun pulsed, and I repeated, "Natalia," to the quiet house.

In the library a single lamp was on. On the coffee table there was a half-empty glass of water on a bamboo coaster. The air vents rumbled, and the furnace began to blow its warm breath through the house.

Back in the kitchen, I leaned on the counter. My elbow brushed the toothpick. I took it to the trash. When I lifted the trashcan lid, I saw it was stuffed with bundles of dried flowers. I went to the garage. The white door to the basement was open. I walked down the steps and wilted to the floor.

I saw my hands against her body. They were etiolated like light-starved leaves. She lay on her side, and the ladder lay parallel to her. In her hand was a bouquet of dried flowers, the blooms a shattered spill of colors trickling away, and her amber eyes seemed to be looking at this destruction patterned with irremeable finality. I gazed into her face, but her eyes were motionless. Then the tears began, and I made a pathetic plea against what had already happened. "No," I said. "No."

Like a sike, I had hope that these tear ducts would dry when again the rays of light between June solstice and autumnal equinox beat down upon my face, or maybe the spring rains would come unabated before then and wash away my life in its deluge, even when I would have expected the world to eventually brighten. There is, however, no fatidical almanac of emotion's weather.

She died of a ruptured tumor. She and the ladder fell, somehow, and when she hit the ground, it cracked open the tumorous, blood-filled growth that her beautiful body contained, buried like an ancient wastepool among the dead eggs of her ovaric chamber. Unconscious from the fall and hemorrhaging within, Natalia's heart pumped for life and bled her to death.

Natalia's parents arrived in time to help with the final arrangements for the funeral. I felt myself floating down a river of ice, looking up into the bright, featureless winter sky, soaked to the bone in freezing water. Thaddeus washed dishes in the kitchen sink downstairs. I heard Cheryl whispering to Jesse in his bedroom. My clothes set out for the next day, I had nothing to do but choose which wall to stare blankly at. I decided on the east wall, and I thought about Mecca and its sacred Black Stone. I thought of Vatican City where reigned the mouthpiece of God, and I thought of men and women in rare churches of the South, dancing with rattlesnakes and cottonmouths in their raised hands. How happy to be one of them, any of them, to have so much surety in grief.

Cheryl rapped on my open door.

"Come in," I said.

"Jesse's in bed now. You should get to bed too. You'll want sleep for the wake tomorrow."

"A sleep for the wake. A wake for her sleep. A wake. A sleep. Awake. Asleep."

"What?"

"Puns. Homophones. Euphemisms. Pestering words. You know." I looked her in the eyes finally and said, "Language constructs our view of these things. We layer what's unpleasant with less sinister words. Death becomes *sleep* becomes *passing on* and then just *gone*. It's all the same thing. The same awful fact. And we soften it."

"There's nothing wrong with describing the loss of a loved one in euphemisms. The reality is harsh enough."

"No, there isn't anything wrong with that. Not at all. Not at all. The problem," I chuckled, "is that I know damn well how we elude the death fact. Make it pretty. Words for me are incapable of softening the hurt. Dampening the blow. I know their twists and turns. Their etymological roots, how they came into being. How they replaced older language, fashioned new meanings out of the corpses of dead words."

"A sage of language. You've always been that."

"A decrepit old man, hunched over his dusty books."

"A man who still loves my daughter. This pain is normal, Robert. It's not easier on me for all the words I take for granted."

"No. I guess I didn't mean to imply that. I wish, though, they could be used as an assuagement for me. It's not easier for you, but you can be comforted by words. That's why we have these euphemisms, these sayings. Unfortunately, they just trouble me the more."

"If you say so." She turned toward the door. Then she turned back. "You've thought a lot on death. It haunts you, this thing that's loomed over your family for so long. Tomorrow. Tomorrow we celebrate her life." Yes, Natalia had wanted not a traditional wake, not a viewing, but a celebration—a gathering of her friends and family. All last looks at her would be done at the funeral the day after the wake. "Then we can lay her to rest and we'll mourn, and in mourning we begin to heal."

"I've never been one for moving on."

Cheryl hugged me. "I feel for you, Robert." She pulled away and there were tears running down her face. "You're right. You'll have the worst of it. More than Jesse even. It's not words, though, that are my comfort. It's my faith in the place where her spirit has gone."

I nodded. What more could I do?

I went to Jesse's room and sat down on his bed beside him. "How are you doing?" I asked.

"I miss Mom," he said.

"I do too," I sighed. "Now we both need to sleep. We've a busy day tomorrow. Lots of mommy's and daddy's friends are going to be at the wake."

"Why?"

"Because it's tradition to do this, to get together and share memories and stories before the burial. Being together in sadness makes the loss less lonely."

"I don't want to be sad."

"Me either, but I am."

"Me too," he said. "Dad, where is Mom?"

I looked at him, my child, snuggled up in blankets while his mother lay dressed for her funeral in the cold vault of a morgue. "She's in a place of peace," I said, and I felt like a liar, even though I could not be sure a liar I was.

I kissed him and shut the lights off and closed his door, and in the click of the latch, I thought I heard his words grope deliberately in the suddenness of dark: "Where is that?"

They stepped through the doorway, wearing scarves and their Sunday best. All friends and family were invited to the house to talk of what had been and how sad, how sudden, and how it was a shame, and how it was a graceful end compared to the slow, painful death that could have been. Most would also show up the next day at the funeral to be held at a Methodist church. Many who stepped through the door spotted flower arrangements in vases they recognized as their own gifts, flowers that had spoken of a hope for healing, though the hope had been little, and the sorrow they felt was all the more wrenching when they saw their vases full of wilted flowers at her wake.

Glasses clinked. The spaces of the house filled with sounds of shuffling feet. The guests swirled through the rooms: the library, the living room, and trickled slow past the area where Natalia's art hung on the walls. They spoke to each other and to me. My responses came out as though from a planchette pressed by circumstance's ghostly fingers. What could anyone say that could contain anything but another bump to jar consciousness into thinking of its sorrow? So I let the talk trickle by like splats of rainwater against the window. They went tap, tap, tap, but it was all a din of gloom with no individual meaning; here my own tongue was but an Illyrian babble in my ears.

I kept looking for Jesse and I'd find him and ask, "How are you doing?"

He'd reply, "Okay," and then he'd be off, dragged into conversing with some friend or hugging a family member.

Warm apple cider was served in the kitchen. A woman with short, curly hair insisted I have some. She ladled me up a cup. I thought of the pumpkin patch and old dog buried there on those grounds. "We're all so upset. So sad, all of us, really. How we'll manage without her, I don't know. We've barely been able to during her absence. So good with those kids. We could use extra art supplies, of course. She said you're not a painter or anything, right? A professor of linguistics?"

"Yes," I said, hardly following her chatter and blowing on my cider. I watched the steam glide across the dark surface of the liquid.

"Here," she said and took my cup and hers and set them on the counter. She put her hands on my own. "We could really use them if you don't have a need."

Was she asking me to donate art supplies to the school? I looked at her and said, "Sure, there's paint brushes, tracing paper. A lot of things."

"Thank you," she said and gave me a deplorable hug.

I turned and walked off without my drink. I slid past Cheryl, who embraced a teary-eyed aunt of Natalia's. I heard Thaddeus's sad laugh bouncing from somewhere. As I scooted by, I saw Porter standing solemnly next to his wife. Reaching the door to Natalia's studio, I stepped in and pulled the door shut. Her blank canvas still rested on the easel, proof there was one more uncreated dream. It was intangible, like the static of space between the stars and galaxies; incomplete—there were no hands to paint the reality which could have dwelled there.

I stepped up to the canvas and observed its empty surface. An audible clearing of a throat sounded behind me. I turned. "Don't care for crowds either?"

"Only in the classroom," I said.

"Sorry if I'm not supposed to be in here."

"It's okay," I said. "How are you, Elizabeth?"

"Good. Last semester, then I've got my PhD." Elizabeth was a former student of mine. She wore a black formal dress. Her hair was cut askew; the longer side had a streak of purple in the front. Bright studio lights glinted off the piercings in her nose and lip. "If you need to be alone—" she said.

"I'll have overmuch aloneness soon enough, won't I?"

She gave me a sympathetic smile. Then she walked over to me, and we stood there in silence, looking at the canvas. It was white, blank, a nothingness that lacked even the liquid emptiness of a black representation of existence; this white *voided* representation of existence, as if the final layer had been stripped and nothing more could be peeled away.

"I'd tell you she's in a better place," she nudged me with her elbow, "but you know that isn't it. Tomorrow she'll be back where it all began. Back in the earth."

"Nothing more?"

"Nothing more germane, professor. It's what you said once. I actually memorized this quote of yours from my lecture notes and use it in conversation on occasion. I hope you don't mind. You said, 'It doesn't matter if it contains seventy-two virgins, golden fields of endless splendors, or shadowy pits full of restless souls, all descriptions of Heaven will pass with time and with succeeding generations. The only fact that is certain is interment, disposal: the long mahogany box, the funeral pyre, the inheritable urn. And like these tangible traces, the words we use to describe death fade. *Acalen. Endedæg. Faeicscipe. Gastlic gast. Endeleasness.* All our descriptions of the *eterne* fall short because all language lasts but a little while. *Handhwile.*'"

"But I've to contend with her box while I live."

Elizabeth put her arm around me and said, "No one would want you to quit struggling with the fact of it, to forget it. Not ever while you're around to remember."

*   *   *

Baptized with water at birth. Baptized with earth at death. Baptized with fire in the afterlife. Ancient rituals spoken in our modern tongue. A few great thinkers were responsible for the world's major technological changes, and the changes make the present landscape, though man, in general, is stubborn, or, perhaps, man is simply built to be devout. Murders have been committed over women. Nations have fought for their respective godrights. Devoted, we engage in these rituals of marriages and funerals, unions and wars. That's what we are, creatures of devotion, a social animal who builds cultures based upon the attachments we have to one another. What better place to show my devotion for Natalia than in a church? Birth rites, death rites, marriage rites, and worshipful acts toward God are all held in these structures designated by special symbols and sacred architectural design. Such buildings are lodestones for devotion.

It was a modern Methodist church. Classrooms and a small religious library were all located in a wing that stretched away from the sanctuary. The sanctuary felt larger than it really was with a vaulted ceiling and a theme of light-grained woods. The windows were high and the glass was not stained. There were two rows of pews, split by an aisle that ran from the narthex to the altar. Between altar and the apse, a Jesusless cross hung from the ceiling. It was white and suspended by wires, engilded by discreet lights affixed to the east wall. On the opposite wall, above the door between nave and narthex, hung a little wooden cross with a dying Jesus. It was funny how the death of God could only be viewed by turning away from the sermon. But perhaps that was the point. Look back toward death, look forward to this symbol of eternal life. Or maybe I was seeing metaphors where they didn't exist, looking for them hanging around and everywhere before me.

While Natalia and I had never been to the church, it was the same denomination that she had been baptized into as a baby, and the church was more than willing to hold the funeral of this local schoolteacher. The religious burial was done in deference to her parents' desire. For me, burying her in the tradition that comforted her parents could not hurt. For Cheryl and Thaddeus, having their daughter's last rites in the church, rather than in some neutral funeral home, would help them heal.

Bright flowers scented the air. Everyone wore black. The pastor was a woman, my age, with a wide and reassuring smile. She came up to me and Natalia's parents and whispered some words to us. We proceeded to her casket for our final viewing, for our final goodbye.

I looked down at Natalia's face. She was beautiful. She was young. The sun would still rise after this rosewood box was locked and lowered into the earth. Stars would continue to twinkle at night. I would have dreams of her as if she were alive. Some things were painful. Other things unfair.

From my pocket, I took a paintbrush I had found in a pile of old brushes she'd uncharacteristically decided not to clean. The bristles were dried together. The last color she had dipped the sable hairs into was a shade of red. I tucked the paintbrush under her hands. Jesse clung to me, rubbed his wet face on my pants. I lifted him and let him give a final kiss. Her parents each whispered in her ear. I tried to say farewell, but the words caught in my throat, and my tears began streaming down hot, like grief itself was burning feverishly inside me. The lid was shut. We moved to the front pew, reserved for us.

The pastor spoke from the pulpit to the left of the altar. She began, "A painter, an assemblagist, and an educator. A mother, a wife, and a daughter."

A little later we were driven to the cemetery. In the earth, a space had been made to receive her. The clouds made a procession across the sky in icy ribbons. The casket was lowered. I shoveled some dirt, symbolically, into her grave, and then I helped Jesse do the same. I stood looking at her headstone, accustoming myself to the widower's stance and the view, knowing I'd be looking at it the same way for many years to come. "If only you could paint this now," I said.

Then the funeral was over. Everyone got in their cars and drove back to their homes. We did the same, even though it felt wrong to leave her there so far from us, entombed atop that gravesite hill.

"Take what you want."

"You can keep the snowman painting," Cheryl said.

"Yeah," I nodded. "I'm thinking I'll rotate them around more often now. But I'll leave this one up for Christmas."

"The one with the clouds there, we'll take that."

"It is really nice," Thaddeus said.

"There's more in the studio."

All three of us walked down the hallway, which creaked with hollow vacancy beneath us. I pulled open the door to her studio, and we went from painting to painting, from project to project. There was so much artwork she had created: collages, prints, drawings, things made of Popsicle sticks and glue. All of it hers and all of it spoke of her diversity of interests, her dedication to art and art education. Looking at the paintings was especially like looking at remnants of her mind, and it gave us much to talk about.

"That's curious." Thaddeus pointed.

"It's a self-portrait," I said. "Her last painting."

Cheryl put her arm around Thaddeus.

"The title is *Woman with Cancer.*"

"What will you do with it?" Cheryl asked.

"It's special. I thought about a museum. I've decided against it though; she wouldn't have liked that. I want to frame it and hang it in the library. Give it a permanent place."

"That's good," Thaddeus nodded.

"It'll be Jesse's someday," I said.

They stayed just over two weeks to get things in order and to grieve and make sure Jesse and I were going to be okay. Thaddeus was especially helpful for Jesse. He sat with him every night and read to him. Thaddeus spoke to him in only the way a grandfather could, offering words to comfort while making him strong. When they left, they left with a carful of things to remind them. I imagined how, spread around their house, her objects, be it her necklace or a picture she painted, would turn their place into a shrine, they the caretakers of these relics of their progeny, their scion branched, flowered, and already withered away.

The world was dull underneath an overcast sky that spit a cold drop, now and then, upon the earth. The shifting noises of silence occupied our abode. It was the first day we sat in it alone, a brace of broken hearts trying to be strong enough to carry the soul of the house into continuation. With her passing, though, the soulful warmth that made our house a home felt aspirated into the outer air, or even farther, into that which is beyond the factual universe.

I sat at the kitchen table, Jesse upstairs. The spoon in my cup clinked against my ceramic mug.

Nothing kept happening. The hushed noises kept building up. They kept layering, filling, and seeping out of the hollow walls themselves. I waited for the noises, quantitatively potent, to burst forth into something tangible. Half the day had gone by. The culmination aching in the walls was near. Then I heard his two feet thump, and he ran down the stairs, and he ran past me and out the door without jacket or shoes. I followed him to the lake. He stood at its shore, watching the water, which reflected the gloom-colored sky and rippled with drops of rain. He cried and he shook and he watched. I came up behind him and put my arms around his shoulders. I did not say anything. We stood there a long time— the rain becoming denser—watching the water. We watched it dance, we watched even after his tears had stopped. Our eyes strained, looking at the lake as it shivered with raindrops and wild ripples, waves jumping out unexpectedly, and we stared at the undulating lake for as long as we could in the cold, but nothing from the depths surfaced, and it, among other things, remained a mystery.

Acknowledgments

I am embarrassed to say how much help I have had for such a short work. *Descriptions of Heaven* had been the longest piece I'd written, and a large number of my friends were quite eager to read my early drafts. I was expecting few critical responses; instead, I received many. For their great comments, questions, and editorial advice, I thank Brenda Johnson, Nolan Peterson, Ashley Hall, Teniesha Kessler, and Kristin Olson. I am indebted to my best friend Mike Convery who encouraged me from the book's conception to its publication. Special thanks to Libby Sturgeon who kept me sane during the publication process and whose keen editorial eye caught excesses and absences that I, and everyone else, had missed. I love you Libs. Much thanks also goes to Martine Bellen, my editor, for helping with the final polish on this novella. I'd like to acknowledge Charlene Eska for her invaluable help in correcting my Old and Middle English. I cannot express enough gratitude to my mom and dad for giving me a space with a large desk from which to write this book. Lastly, I wish to thank anyone who I may have forgotten to mention here but whose comments impacted the final form of this work.

**More books from
Harvard Square Editions:**

People and Peppers, Kelvin Christopher James

Gates of Eden, Charles Degelman

Love's Affliction, Fidelis Mkparu

Transoceanic Lights, S. Li

Close, Erika Raskin

Anomie, Jeff Lockwood

Living Treasures, Yang Huang

Leaving Kent State, Sabrina Fedel

Dark Lady of Hollywood, Diane Haithman

How Fast Can You Run, Harriet Levin Millan

A Cat Came Back, Simone Martel

Nature's Confession, J.L. Morin

No Worse Sin, Kyla Bennett

Stained, Abda Khan